FIRST XI

Born in Wisbech, Cambridgeshire in 1948, Bob Cattell has written a number of children's books about sport including the popular *Glory Gardens* cricket series. Others include the *Strikers* football books and the *Butter-Finger* trilogy written with poet John Agard. The royalties from his latest book, *Bowl like the Devil*, have been donated to the cricketing charity Chance to Shine.

First XI is his first book of fiction for adult readers and reflects a lifetime's passion for the game of cricket.

FIRST XI

Eleven stories of the world of cricket

Bob Cattell

illustrations by
Bob Linney

Charlcombe Books
17 George's Road, Bath BA1 6EY
Tel 01225-335813

First published 2015

ISBN 978 0 9568510 5 5

Cover design by Bill Jackson

Printed and bound in Great Britain by
CPI Antony Rowe, Bumper's Farm, Chippenham, Wilts

Contents

To the memory of Neil Russell

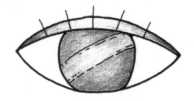

RUN
Australia

'I'm the only Australian here. All the rest of you are immigrants.' How many times had she heard him say that? Her grandpa never tried to hide his roots. Far from it... 'Abo and proud of it.' And when it came to cricket he was ever quick to introduce you to the Hall of Fame, starting with Eddie Gilbert and Jack Marsh.

As a young girl Chrissie had listened spellbound as he recounted the exploits of Albert Henry, 'the fastest bowler ever seen', and of the remarkable Black Lords, the first Australian cricket team to tour England. She knew the names of all of them off by heart: Johnny Mullagh, Jim Crow, Sundown... although Grandpa usually insisted on giving them all their proper names: Unaarrimin, Jallachmurrimin, Ballrinjarrimin.

They played 47 games in England in 1868. Packed houses, especially the day they played Surrey and Mullagh scored 73 in 80 minutes. A clever performance and worthy of any batsman, no matter what his country or colour, wrote the Sporting Gazette. There were three matches a week – 19 draws, 14 losses and 14 wins.

On top of that they put on popular entertainments for the crowds. One of their number, Dick-a-Dick – Junganjinuke, Grandpa called him – would dodge and defend himself from cricket balls pelted at him from point blank range with only a narrow war shield and a curved club called a leangle for protection. And the only Englishman ever to beat them in a throwing competition was a certain WG Grace.

The tour seems to have been a great success, in spite of the poor weather. They are perfectly civilised and are quite familiar with the English language, reported the Times. History, however, has nothing to say about who took the profits. 'They must have been bloody tired when they got on the boat at the end of that summer,' said Grandpa.

He also told her about the time when Gilbert bowled Bradman for a duck. And the racism that kept many good players – men and women – out of the national team.

Now there would be no more stories. Grandpa was gone at 99. He'd have been disappointed to miss out on his century had he not been pretty well absent in his mind these past three years. He had died peacefully in his sleep.

It wasn't her first encounter with death. Her eldest brother, Jack, had died in a car crash not two years ago. His body had been buried and for months she'd been haunted by the thought of the worms consuming him, the mould corrupting his young face, the hideous images of decay. To Chrissie's relief, her grandfather's body was to be cremated. She knew he was ready to die and she was almost pleased for him. Her chief regret was that she'd never been able to tell him she'd been picked to play for Australia.

It was a bright sunny morning and a good crowd was massing outside the church, the men uncomfortably warm in their suits; the women wearing cotton dresses and big hats. Grandpa had agreed to a church funeral because he said that's what everyone else would want. He wasn't a church man himself, even though he'd married a Catholic. After a drink he'd sometimes say there are three words to describe Roman Catholics, and 'Roman' and 'Catholics' are two of them.

As a young child Chrissie had once seen him talking to a large rock over by one of their favourite picnic places. He told her the Rainbow Serpent had left it there when he passed through in the Creation Period. But by and large he kept what beliefs he had to himself. They were likely tied up with his wanderings and no-one knew where he went or what he did. He called it 'going on the run'.

"Been walkabout, mate?" his friends would ask him.

"Nah. I been on the run. Handed myself in again yesterday."

Now he was on the run for good. He'd never once mentioned the idea of having a traditional native burial ceremony and besides there was no-one left on his side of the family now to carry it out.

Chrissie listened to the buzz of the crowd nervously. Half the town seemed to be there. For all his outspokenness and erratic behaviour Grandpa had been a popular man: a good neighbour, a charmer, especially with the women, and for many years a regular at the cricket club bar and most of the other bars around town. In his youth, they said, he'd been a fist fighting man following a few beers. An exuberant batsman, too; still the holder of the record for the town's fastest 50. But that was before Chrissie was born; she had witnessed none of his wilder adventures.

"I am very sad for you, Chrissie. I know how close you were, you and your Grandfather."

It was Mrs Foyle, the headmaster's wife. Last of the bloody colonials, Grandpa called her. They had been his next-door neighbours for many years until he moved to the sheltered flat in town. At school Chrissie developed a similar distaste for her and her pompous husband, 'Lardy' Foyle.

"He was an honest man," she said.

"Well… yes," said Mrs Foyle. "Honest to a fault."

Why the hell have you come? thought Chrissie. Why visit your mean moralising on his last rites, you old cow?

People began to drift into the church and take their seats. She pulled herself together but her nervousness grew. She wiped the palms of her hands on her dress, tried to keep her mind clear. Her mother had asked her to say a few words about Grandpa and she'd agreed instinctively but now she was beginning to wonder whether she had the strength to stand up in front of all those people and say what she wanted to say.

Her mother led her to their place in the front stall. She smelt the incense and heard the priests, swishing to and fro in their long robes and arranging their books and other mysteries of their calling. It was cool in the church and when the organ started playing she felt herself relax a little.

She kept thinking that Grandpa would have no time for this. He'd never taken to the bloody Roman rigmarole as he called it. Her mother was a staunch Catholic, her dad had been confirmed in the church but was not much of a church-goer. That had been a help to Chrissie when she stopped going herself and had to face her mother's wrath and disappointment. Her dad, two brothers and a cousin were waiting outside. They were the coffin bearers and would enter during the course of the first hymn. Her mother had chosen it: *To be a pilgrim*. It was sort of appropriate for Grandpa who was forever off on his wanders, usually leaving someone somewhere in the lurch.

The choir was in good voice today. After depositing the coffin her father and brothers joined Chrissie and her mother in the pew. Her dad's deep bass voice boomed out the words: *Hobgoblin nor foul fiend can daunt his spirit. He knows he at the end will life inherit. Then fancies flee away…* The strange words filled her with comfort.

Prayers followed and the priest spoke about life and death and resting places. Her elder brother read a lesson from St Matthew. It began: *Lay not up for yourselves treasures upon earth, where moth and rust doth corrupt.* And then suddenly it was her turn. The priest approached. "Chrissie are you ready?" he said softly and led her by the arm to the lectern. She tapped the mike as her brother had done, stared ahead and began in a strong voice.

"I'm a quarter Australian and three quarters immigrant," she said with a wry smile. There was a brief silence and then her father chuckled and a ripple of laughter ran through the church as everyone recognised the source of her words.

"I want to tell you a story that Grandpa told me. It's about a cricketer. One of the fastest bowlers Australia has ever seen. But don't take my word for it. This is what Sir Donald Bradman said about him: "He sent down the fastest bowling I can remember, one delivery knocked the bat out of my hand and I unhesitatingly class this short burst faster than anything seen." Who was he talking about? Larwood? Voce? No. It was Eddie Gilbert, Eddie born not a hundred miles away from here at a place called Durundur in south Queensland, the son of two Kanji people. He played 23 games for Queensland. With his long arms he achieved the astounding pace the Don talked about. He had a sort of slinging action like Jeff Thomson or Mitchell Johnson. And he clean bowled Bradman with his fifth ball that day. Grandpa called it 'the biggest mistake of his life'. It propelled Eddie into the limelight. And there were a lot of people who didn't like that.

"Because as a black cricketer Eddie didn't play on a level playing field. He had to get permission from the Protector every time he was chosen to represent his state. He couldn't travel with his Queensland teammates and he often had to stay in separate accommodation.

"In 1931 in Melbourne, he was no-balled 11 times in three overs for throwing. Strange that. Because in his next game, umpired by George Hele, who officiated in the Bodyline series, he was not no-balled a single time. But nevertheless from that moment on he had to battle with persistent suspicions about his action. That and illness accounted for his short first-class career, which saw him take 87 wickets at an average of 28.97, including six five-wicket hauls. In 1934/35 he took 9 for 178 against New South Wales and 5 for 77 against Victoria. And for those matches, although granting him permission to play, the Protector refused to pay his expenses.

"The more the officials made life difficult for him, the more the fans loved him. But they didn't make the decisions. In November 1936, Eddie Gilbert was given his marching orders from the game and sent back to his settlement. Queensland CC even demanded the return of his cricket clothes. He died near Brisbane in January 1978. Bradman, to his credit, attended his funeral."

She stopped speaking and listened to the silence, with the occasional intake of breath.

"Grandpa said that he, personally, had been lucky. He lived in an age when racism and prejudice were on the decline. It would never go away completely, of course, because some folks can't abide difference... it kind of threatens their very existence. But the way Grandpa lived his life was a testimony to honesty. He never stopped being an Aborigine – that's what he called himself as you all know. An Abo living in a very strange and changing society and being true to himself and his heritage. That's what I hope I've learned from him. And that's why as long as I live he'll be here for me and in me."

The priest led her back to the pew. Her dad patted her knee. "Proud of you," he whispered.

Outside the church the family stood in line as the mourners passed and offered their condolences. Her mother asked each of them, one by one, back to the house for the wake. A wake was one of the few good ideas to have come out of the Irish Catholic church, Grandpa said.

Someone stopped next to her and took her hand. "That was a brave speech. Very brave." Mrs Foyle again.

"Brave?"

"Can't have been easy for you… not being able to see anyone."

"On the contrary. It made it easier to concentrate on what I was saying."

"Really? Well anyway, good luck with your cricket match. To be honest I'd never heard of blind cricket till I read about it in the paper. Playing for Australia, fancy that. Blind cricket!"

CUT
Sri Lanka

My name is Henry Claasen. My friends call me 'Cutter', a nickname that comes from my early cricket playing days when the cut shot was practically the only attacking stroke that I mastered. I had then and still have an array of cut shots: the late cut, the square cut, the cut drive, the aerial or upper cut and the – possibly unique – reverse cut which until recently was my only scoring shot on the leg side.

I am, what we call in Sri Lanka, a Burgher, a mixed race descendent of the European colonialists, in my case of Dutch origin. There have been Claasens in Sri Lanka since the eighteenth century. My wife was a Tamil, a fact that created some friction with my parents because they had someone from the Burgher community lined up for me. They didn't realise that boundaries were on the move in those days. Having sent me to Charterhouse to be scarred for life by the unique cruelty of an English boarding school education, they wanted an altogether better return on their investment than what I became: a prawn farmer and a happy family man.

Lanya and I lived in Galle. The prawn and lobster farm was further east at Dondra and the growing demand from the hotels and restaurants on the south coast turned it into a thriving business. We had a daughter, Malinda. She was six in 2004 – an only child because I was diagnosed with cancer soon after her birth and operations and chemo got in the way of a bigger family. The procedures were ultimately successful in so much as there has so far been no reappearance of the tumour. But in those years I talked rather too much about my funeral which, I suppose, made me more aware of what Lanya would have wanted. She and Malinda died in the tsunami, on the train from Colombo to Galle. Days later Lanya's body was recovered from a carriage, Malinda's was never found. It was the worst rail disaster in history with nearly 2,000 deaths. Only in Sri Lanka do you get 2,000 people dying on a train. A further 200,000 died on the south coast that dreadful day.

The funeral was the simple family affair that I insisted on. Just very close family and two friends who each read a poem, one in English, the other in Tamil. Apart from the poems which I know off by heart I don't remember a great deal about the funeral and the days that followed. At first, the shock of it completely numbed me. If my wife and daughter hadn't died I'd have got along fine in my life, happily adjusting to minor squalls. But when they were gone the tempest of their deaths left me barely afloat.

Nevertheless I tried hard to find an anchorage. My business and most of the people who worked for it had been completely wiped out by the wave and I had neither the resources nor the energy to build it up again. In a forlorn attempt to hold on to the memory of Lanya and Malinda I threw myself into many tasks for rebuilding the communities of the south coast. I raised money, organised shipments of food, helped to run a private bus service, co-ordinated a reconstruction programme for the fishing communities and finally set up my own charity. It was at this time I met Muttiah... but I'll come to him later.

In a whirlwind of activity I also started playing chess again – I had been quite a good player when I was young and had won a few tournaments and competitions. I also took up running. Sometimes I would run a hundred or more kilometres a week. But none of this frenetic activity brought the peace I craved.

I was drifting. Every day I would wake up in the morning and launch myself furiously into the hours ahead and find the same black hole every night. The few women I met seemed to sense my sadness and strangeness and they quickly changed course before there was any chance of a relationship getting started. In short, I lacked the projection for launching myself into a new life. But I got used to it, month after month, year after year. And then Rajendra came along and everything was turned on its head.

Today, as I walk along Maitland Crescent towards the Nondescripts' Cricket Club Ground I am smiling… thinking of the upheaval, the chaos, we have both been through. It is a late April morning, the winter rains over and the heat of Colombo beginning to build up. It will get much hotter in the months to come. Piles of mangoes and pineapples have started to appear on the street stalls and their sweet fragrance hangs in the air. I quicken my pace. I promised Raj that I'd be there to watch his first game for Nondescripts but I've been unavoidably held up at the office. The game will have started… nearly an hour ago. I pray I haven't missed the chance to see him bowl his very first over in first-class cricket.

Rajendra came to live with me almost exactly two years ago. He was the son of Lanya's youngest brother, who had been killed in the last months of the fighting in the north. I don't think he was directly involved with the Tamil Tigers but you can never tell – the propaganda from both sides in the war obscured reality like layers of thick, opaque varnish. After his father's death, Rajendra spent 18 months in a detention camp in Vavuniya District. When he was released he discovered his mother had died, too. So, to cut a long story short, I agreed to sponsor him and he came to live with me in Colombo. It was the very least I could do for my wife's family. But I didn't know what I was letting myself in for.

Badly damaged by the death of his parents and the trauma of the detention camp, Raj was practically silent for the first few months of his stay. He was 15 when he arrived. I found him a place in a reasonably good school and tried to get him interested in picking up on his studies again. He was a bright boy but he seemed unable to connect. He missed more days at school than he attended and made no friends. Most of his time was spent playing games on the mobile phone that I regretted giving him. That's when he wasn't smashing up his bedroom or throwing his dinner at me or threatening to attack me with a bread knife.

I tried hard to talk to him about his experiences in the camp. He made some elliptical reference to torture and brutality and then clammed up completely on the subject. Nevertheless I was aware of his hatred for his captors and the Sri Lankan army and, by association, everything non-Tamil. He told me more than once that he reserved a special hatred for half-caste Burgers. That was just to get at me, of course.

His behaviour was becoming increasingly dangerous. The government was quick to spot any tendency towards terrorism and Colombo was still awash with agents and informers. I tried a psychiatrist, a counsellor. I talked to his teachers, introduced him to my friends, found part-time jobs for him working with my charity. But the silent evenings and weekends continued.

If we did talk it was only to argue and fight. I can see now that we were both angry about our respective fates. Raj was too sharp to let me get away with preaching at him.

"You'll have a better chance of surviving if you learn to tolerate loss," I said to him on one occasion.

"What am I hearing?" he sneered.

"Put it behind you. Start afresh."

"And leave you to wallow in your self-pity all on your own?"

That was the closest I came to hitting him. Probably because it was true. But I refused to hear what he was saying, although I'm sure I began to understand it in some burgeoning part of myself. As for him, nothing, it seemed, could entice him out of the bleak and angry place in which he had taken refuge.

And then something did. I had by this time given up chess and running and had just started playing cricket again. A week after my 50th birthday, which I now know is a dangerous time in any man's life, I met some friends – veterans like myself – and, together with a few younger players who could run about in the field for us, we launched a cricket team to play charity matches. We get the occasional celebrity or top cricketer to play for us to boost takings for the charity. It's a wandering side… we challenge clubs all over the island and usually lose to them though no-one can fault us for a lack of competitiveness.

Right from the start we had a Thursday evening ritual of practice nets at the Nondescript ground, which we gained access to because one of our team was a great friend of the president of the club.

One Thursday, in another attempt to get Raj to stop moping around, I asked him to come with me to nets. To my great surprise, he agreed. He'd never shown any interest in cricket before.

I was batting when Nick Ondatje, our medium pace opening bowler persuaded Raj to have a go at bowling. Seeing him run up to the wicket I decided to defend the delivery with a show of great respect. And – whatever he bowled – praise him for it in front of the others. Rajendra is quite short for his age and stocky. He doesn't look much like a bowler. He ran in, fast for a spinner, off half a dozen paces, gave the ball plenty of air and I went forward to meet it. It dipped, drifted towards my pads, fizzed off the matting and took out my off stump. I'd been done by the perfect doosra. I and the rest of the team were speechless. Raj allowed himself a quiet smile as he calmly picked up another ball to bowl again.

Then everyone was laughing and talking to him – ruffling his hair, patting him on the back, encouraging him to bowl at me again. He did… and had me lbw, caught behind and bowled again in quick succession. And I wasn't the only batter to suffer humiliation that evening.

After nets it was our custom to have a quick drink in the Cricket Club Cafe just round the corner. Rajendra came under fire from a barrage of questions. Where did he learn to bowl? Who taught him the doosra? How did he get so much rotation on the ball? And would he play for us? At first he shrugged off the cross examination in his usual silent manner. But slowly he opened up. He had loved cricket at school, although with the disruption of the war he'd had no opportunity to play for a club. In the detention camp he had played almost every day with the other lads. Murali had, of course, been his hero. He was the hero of every Tamil boy… and most of the other aspiring cricketers on the island, too. Raj was utterly determined to bowl like Murali and he sought out one of the detainees in the camp who had been a cricket coach to help him with his dream. He said that he bowled for as long as he could every day. Usually at a single stump or a branch stuck in the ground.

I didn't tell Raj at that time that I knew Muttiah Muralitharan. We had worked together on several projects after the tsunami. Murali was tireless in the effort he put in for the devastated fishing villages and he gained huge respect. Unlike many other volunteers, he stayed on board long after the media had moved on to feast on other world disasters. I only had to pick up the phone and suggest a new project to him and he would be there. And he wasn't just a figure head… he'd be standing in the trucks loading sacks or carrying bricks to a new building site.

Rajendra played several games for us. Thanks to him we won most of them which was a refreshing, new experience for the team. The fund-raising did well out of it too, as word got round and more and more people came to see him bowl. But I knew he was too good for us… that he needed to move on to a higher standard of cricket. So I rang Murali and asked him to come along and take a look. And I decided to keep his visit a secret from Raj.

The evening Murali turned up at the Nondescripts' net was a turning point in the relationship between Raj and me. When Raj realised his guardian was a friend of his hero he dropped the last of his defences. We were already getting closer because of the cricket, but this was the final bond. I realised that I had changed too. For the first time in ten years I saw my place in the unforgiving world less as a catalogue of random events, good and bad, but rather as a life – both abstract and finite. My relationship with Rajendra and my growing fatherly love for him, in spite of what we had been through, had allowed me to cross a line. '*My heart went out to thee for thy charity and thy courtesy and the wisdom of thy little years,*' said the old Lama to Kim in the book which I re-read every year. Till now there had been precious little charity and courtesy in Rajendra's attitude to me... but that was about to change.

Murali spent most of the evening patiently signing autographs for the kids who had snuck into the ground once the news got out that he was there. But he still found time to chat to the players, none of whom had met him before, and to give Raj some tips about his bowling. Over the following weeks he frequently offered Raj a spell of coaching. He told me with a facetious grin that the lad was the best spin bowling prospect since Shane Warne came out of Australia.

It didn't take long before Nondescripts invited Raj to play for their second XI. And after a month he got his chance with the first team, appropriately against the Tamil Union club.

The ground is looking immaculate. Fortunately for me Nondescripts are batting and so Raj won't have taken to the field yet. I look around for him and eventually spot him sitting on the middle balcony of the new pavilion. And he's talking to Murali. I feel a pang of guilt that I've failed to arrive on time for this important occasion and that Murali, with all his commitments, has dropped everything to see the boy play.

Nondescripts are in a spot of bother. It's 47 for three after 15 overs. And as I join Raj and Murali another wicket falls to a run out mix up. I apologise for being late and ask why the home team is struggling.

"Early morning dew, Cutter," says Murali. "It's seaming around. But it'll flatten out later."

"What number are you batting?" I ask Raj. He'd be a decent batter if he overcame a tendency to be a bit impulsive.

"Nine," he says. "One more wicket and I'll have to pad up."

Murali was right. The batting got easier. Raj went in on 195 for seven and looked as confident as any player who has been batting at this level all his life. He even cheekily played my signature reverse cut and saluted me with his bat raised high after the ball had raced to the backward-square-leg boundary. He was last out in the final over with the score on 229. He had made 18.

The Tamil Union innings progressed steadily without much incident. I chatted to Muttiah, keeping one eye on Raj fielding alternatively at square-leg and cover-point.

"We had a talk about his first over," said Muttiah, just before Raj comes on to bowl.

"Yes?"

"He needs a plan. Too much variation early on will spoil his rhythm. So we agreed the plan ball by ball. Just for the first over. He must make his own choices after that."

We watched the first ball, a looping off break on a length – leg break to the left-hander. The second beat the batter as he prodded forward and spun over off stump. The third turned sharply again but they ran a bye as the keeper fumbled.

"Fourth ball the doosra," said Murali. "But I wonder if he'll change his plan now he's up against the right hander."

He did. The ball turned sharply into his pads – a stifled appeal but it was going down. A quicker ball followed which the batter dug out just in time.

"Now the doosra," muttered Murali, watching intently and appearing to communicate by telepathy. The look on his face reminded me of those high-charged occasions when his genius snatched victory single handed for Sri Lanka. The Test match at the Oval. 13 wickets against South Africa at Galle. 11 for 110 versus India.

Raj spun himself a catch in the way that reminded everyone of Murali, and ran in. The batter played forward to a dipping delivery and edged straight into the hands of the slip fielder. Raj had his wicket in his first over.

Muttiah leapt to his feet. "Perfect doosra. Couldn't have bowled it better."

More than anyone in Sri Lankan cricket, he stood apart as a source of joy on the field. But as a man Muttiah is much more than that. He could easily have been stigmatised as a Tamil mascot, manipulated by the Sri Lankan state. It's a tribute to him and to the solidarity of his team-mates that he has never been seen in that role. But he has played many others: the proud Tamil in Sri Lanka; Sri Lanka's champion in the lists of world cricket; the greatest spin bowler the world has ever seen. And throughout he has been humble and generous and true to his genius by playing the game year after year with such obvious pleasure. What better role model could any young man ask for?

"You've guided him well," I said to Murali.

"So have you, Cutter," he replied. "He owes it all to you."

SIX
Afghanistan

"Six!" shouted Zahra's brother-in-law, Rachid. He did a little dance round the television, his knees kicking up his shalwar kameez and his arms held high in a wide 'V'.

"Fine shot, Nabi," said her husband, gulping down another gulab.

Zahra smiled. She was delighted that the family of her husband Karim had turned out to be cricket lovers. And now at last they all had something exciting to shout about. Afghanistan had qualified for the T20 World Cup and they were playing India in their first game. And putting up a real fight, too, though, with five wickets already down, Mohammed Nabi was their last chance of an unlikely victory against MS Dhoni and his team of giants.

Zahra had loved cricket for as long as she could remember. She had played in the camp almost as soon as she could get her hands around a taped-up tennis ball. Playing cricket was the highlight of the long day. So often the only highlight. At five o'clock when the summer sun began to lose its fierce heat, the Pakistani aid workers and driver boys would set up their stumps on the flat bit of rubbish-strewn ground down by the Kabul River and the game would begin. The Afghan lads of all ages joined in. At first she was tolerated, as a toddler who would run and run and fetch the ball for them. She loved the way they shouted at her to hurry up and then laughed when she fell over throwing the ball in with all her might.

But soon her catching and throwing and finally her tricky off-spin bowling earned her the respect of the boys. The moment she would never forget came when she clean bowled Mohammed Nabi – yes, the very same Mohammed Nabi who was, even then, the best player of them all. He was young, scarcely a teenager, but you could see he had something different, both as an off-spinner and a clean hitter of the ball. Zahra watched him like a hawk. She learned her bowling action from him – the squeeze of the ball, the high elbows, the loping run of just five steps, the characteristic curl of the arm. And now here he was belting the great Yuvraj Singh for six straight into the upper tiers of the stand in Colombo.

In the camp they played every evening till it got dark throughout the spring and summer. The summers were blisteringly hot and the winters freezing cold and the cheap concrete refugee huts weren't built like a proper Afghan house to resist the extremes of temperature. Her father had taken his family to Peshawar and then to the camp when the mujahideen began to intensify their war against the Russians and life in Kabul became dangerous and then intolerable. Her older brothers, Bashir and Arif, fought with the mujahideen: Bashir died when his group was bombed in the Panjshir Valley.

Zahra had been born in the camp. For the first ten years of her life she knew nothing of Afghanistan except from the stories her mother and grandmother told her. There were few family possessions and no photos of their old life. The family returned to Kabul in the last years of the Taliban's rule. And that was the end of cricket. Girls didn't play cricket in Kabul in those days. The Taliban leaders reluctantly permitted the boys to play as long as they wore beards and celebrated taking wickets with just a polite handshake. How things had changed since then. Hamid Hassan, the young fast bowler, had Afghan flags painted on his cheeks and performed a succession of summersaults whenever he took a wicket. There was even a national women's team with plans to play in international tournaments, though there was still a great deal of opposition to them competing in front of mixed crowds. Zahra knew some of the young women players. One or two of them were good but few had her natural talent. It was too late for her to dream, however.

Life in Kabul was hard after their return. Their house lay in ruins, her father had no job and he and her brother worked for their uncle in his general store. But they rebuilt the house and, after the Americans arrived Arif found work as a driver for the UN. Her heart went dead as she thought of Arif. Lively, funny Arif, always telling his stories about the people he drove across the country and the far-off places he went to. Always ready to laugh about the dangers he faced for what people called taking the Yankee dollar. He had died just over four years ago in a suicide bombing in central Kabul. She saw his mangled body before they buried him. Two brothers destroyed by a stupid war that nobody wanted.

Zahra was married when she was 18 to a jeweller who was exactly 20 years older than her. It was a good marriage for the family but for Zahra it came too soon after the anguish of Arif's death, and she wasn't happy about leaving her family for a strange household. Her husband was quiet, devout and appeared very severe at first. But they both relaxed as they got to know each other. He was hard working and, like most jewellers, comfortably well off. In Kabul that meant 'rich'. She was now six months pregnant with their first child.

"Six!" screamed Rachid. Nabi had hit Zaheer Khan for another enormous blow into the night sky, a cover drive this time, way over the ropes. A massive hit.

Karim smiled at Zahra and continued eating his gulab. "We have a chance of a miracle, maybe," he said.

"If only we'd held our catches we would have won by now," said Rachid.

"Inshallah," said Karim and smiled again.

Zahra smiled back. Her husband was rather fat and getting fatter every day. He now had a double chin and, as he sat cross-legged in front of the television, his blue shalwar kameez rested comfortably on his domed stomach. The problem was his weakness for mithai. He loved the sweet things that Zahra cooked for him: gulab and laddu, halva and jalebi and best of all her kulche badami. Zahra didn't mind him being fat. He reminded her sometimes of her first cricket hero, Inzamam-ul-Haq. Inzi would never have been a successful T20 player because he didn't like to run. He didn't like to field or practice or take any exercise either. But his cover drive was to die for and the way he threaded the ball perfectly between point and cover with that wristy, flowing power was one of the most beautiful things she had witnessed in her life.

Now she worshipped another batter who looked completely different. He was skinny and bald and had a huge beard like a maulana. She had seen only the highlights of Hashim Amla's 300 for South Africa against England that summer at the Oval, but it was enough for her heart to go out to him. He had broken hearts that day: those of Stuart Broad and Jimmy Anderson and the other England bowlers – but such timing, such beauty.

Nabi was now opening his shoulders but taking more chances as the required run rate climbed. Another boundary from a Zaheer full toss, beautifully flicked off his pads to backward square leg for four more precious runs. But he was living dangerously as the run rate climbed. Zahra could hardly bear to watch. She helped herself to some halva and munched it nervously. She didn't normally eat in front of the men, but this was different.

"16 runs off the over!" drooled Rachid. Zahra had never seen him so animated. Rachid's wife, Noreen, looked at him suspiciously as she came in with a tray of chai. She laid it at the feet of the men. Two of her girls, Saira and Sameera, followed her into the room and sat giggling together in the corner. Her youngest child, the nine months old Abbas, was asleep, enveloped in a sling around her shoulders.

"I wish he would get this excited about earning money for his family," she said to Zahra, with a knowing look. It had taken Zahra a long time to get on the right side of Noreen, who was ten years older than her and hadn't taken easily to a younger woman moving into the house. But Noreen had a proper sense of humour, which helped diffuse things, and now the baby was coming and everything had changed. Noreen and Rachid had six children – four girls and two boys. The oldest was eight and Noreen was determined that all of them should have a proper education… which is why she kept on and on at Rachid about earning more money.

She was about to continue her assault when a howl of despair from Rachid stopped her in her tracks. Nabi had holed out to Sharma at mid-off off the bowling of Ashwin.

"All over," said Rachid. "Nabi gone… we can't win."

"But still three wickets left," said Karim.

"Not enough. Not enough"

Rachid was right. The end came in less than three overs. Afghanistan were all out, a mere 23 runs short of their target.

Zahra watched the Indian team congratulating the last two Afghan batters who looked disappointed but accepted the handshakes keenly. It was their first encounter on the big stage and they would never forget it.

"The boys did us proud," said Karim.

"One day we will beat India and Pakistan and even Australia," said Rachid.

Karim leaned forward and placed his hand on Zahra's stomach. "And maybe we win the World Cup when this one plays for his country. He will be a fine player. An all rounder like Nabi."

Zahra shook her head. "No," she said adamantly.

Her husband looked puzzled.

"But *she* will be captain of Afghanistan," she said. And they all laughed.

OFF
England

She'd only half made up her mind to go through with it. Though it had to be said it was the perfect day... warm and not a cloud in the sky.

She couldn't remember the precise moment the idea had come into her head, but that evening with Clare had been a turning point, when she told her friend that Tim had invited her to a Test match at Lord's. Tim was her boyfriend, more than likely a short-term one. He was good-looking and loaded, a hedge fund manager or something of the sort from the City. Not her type normally but he was persistent and very generous. Clare, of course, didn't like him.

The prospect of a day at Lord's had thrilled her. She remembered going to watch Yorkshire with her dad when she was at school. Michael Vaughan had been her favourite but she only saw him bat once – in a one-day game. He was always off playing for England. She liked the rhythm of cricket, although she'd never played it. They didn't do cricket at her school.

She and Clare were students at the LSE, both reading history and politics. They had been friends for two years. Clare didn't share her excitement about a day at Lord's. She said that watching cricket with Tim sounded worse than reading the memoirs of Tony Blair. She couldn't recall how the subject of a streak had cropped up but Clare suddenly got very excited and bet her £50 she wouldn't dare. After a third glass of wine she took the bet.

And now here she was looking out on the beautifully mown ground bathed in sunlight and having second and third thoughts.

The golden age of streaking was long gone. The seventies and eighties were its heyday. Erika Roe at Twickenham – 'Titters at Twickers' screamed the Mirror approvingly. 'Good luck to Erika. She has given the men of Britain a wonderful tonic.' She was snapped from every angle and subjected to all the innuendoes and double-entendres in the Fleet Street lexicon.

Scarcely a Test match went by in those days without someone getting their kit off. It was one of the early streaks that had kindled her interest. Her father was to blame. The moment was memorably described by John Arlott. Arlott died on 14th December 1991, the day of her birth and her dad said they played the scene endlessly on radio and TV all that day... "Not very shapely and it's masculine," purred Arlott in his signature West Country accent. "And I would think it's seen the last of its cricket today."

When much later she heard the commentary on YouTube it came across as a sound bite from a distant era. She bridled at the very English smuttiness. But it reminded of her dad who had died when she was 16. And it laid the germ of an idea.

Since then, almost unconsciously, she had researched the photos, watched the old footage, kept ancient newspaper cuttings. She'd even included a short history of streaking in one of her essays on the early years of feminism, though she had some difficulty explaining its relevance to her tutor.

In the eighties, it seemed to her, things were simpler and streakers were dismissed as just a bit of fun. Now the fines and the security and the big money had taken the spirit out of it… and out of most sport too, some would say. On cricket grounds, streaking vanished along with the antics of the big characters of the game – Botham and Gower and Richards. Gone too were the West Indian supporters knocking out their infectious rhythms on bongos and beer cans. They were replaced by Mexican waves and the Barmy Army and a weird obsession with fancy dress at places such as Headingley and Old Trafford. Semi-nudity was now official anyway. The T20 dancers who celebrated boundaries and wiggled their arses at the fall of wickets provided all the tonic the men of Britain seemed to need nowadays.

But strangely, female nudity still had the power to shock. The tabloids, for all their bums and tits, took a prurient stance on it. Mothers forced art centres to take down 'offensive' nude portraits for fear of them corrupting their offspring. Other mothers were pilloried for breastfeeding in public. Young girls froze their butts off to wear the skimpiest fashions on city centre Saturday nights. It was a confusing but very British response to the female body.

She knew too that nudity could subvert. The Femen movement and their message demonstrated the brave stand that young women could make against the brutality of 21st century kleptocracies. That was what her streak was going to be. That's how she and Clare saw it. A political statement with a hint of irony. And though in her heart of hearts she feared it would miss the mark or be misunderstood, she stood stubbornly by her conviction.

Then there were the counter arguments. Her mother would hate it. It would almost certainly cost her dearly in fines and red tape and she might even get a criminal record. And as she sat in the sunshine waiting for the game to start she began to think the whole thing was ridiculous. She was never going to go through with it, however galling it might be to hand over £50 to Clare.

Tim arrived. And to her mild surprise she found that her day wasn't to be spent in his exclusive company, but with Tim and two of his chums. Brian was another banker, tall, blonde and rather charming... at least until later when he got very drunk and silly. He and Tim spent most of the morning teasing the other chum whose name she never properly picked up – Simon or Stephen or Sebastian – a chinless wonder with a loud, braying laugh that ended in a 'wa...wa...wa'. She was annoyed at Tim for this invasion and instead of settling back to enjoy a good day's cricket she felt increasingly an outsider from the group.

The morning session was rather slow with the bowlers on top, but after two early wickets there had been no further breakthrough. The main excitement seemed to come from the champagne corks which arced regularly over her head to loud cheers and landed on the pitch. Brian told her that one of the stewards had a full-time job picking them up.

At lunch time they made their way to the lawn for a picnic. She surveyed the scene with some amusement. Packed into this little space of greenery under the trees were hundreds of rugs and picnic hampers and tables. The precious picnic pitches had been reserved before the game began, and were now filling up with red-faced men in red trousers and clashing MCC ties, trim matrons from the shires, brash young estate agents noisily pulling the corks from expensive bottles and confident women spreading out their array of Ottolenghi delights. There was scarcely room to squeeze through the masses to their own rug which had been positioned under a tree by Chinless long before she'd arrived. Tim had explained it to her as one of the rituals of the English summer... like strawberries at Wimbledon and hats at Ascot.

She'd already drunk too much champagne but Tim's friends had moved on to Chablis and her glass was filled again. More people joined them: City friends, old college mates. She talked to an Italian man and his blonde English wife. He knew absolutely nothing about cricket.

"72 runs for two out. Is this good?" he asked.

"Difficult to say," said Brian. "Tricky wicket, I think."

"Shan't know what's a good score till England bat," said Tim.

"And when will that be?" asked the Italian.

"Some time tomorrow, probably."

"Tomorrow... mamma mia."

"We're only here today," said the blonde wife with more than a hint of relief in her voice.

"Try the grouse," said Chinless, pushing a large container under her nose stuffed with up to a dozen smelly, brown birds.

"I'll stick to the salmon," she said.

Play restarted at 1.40 but there was no sign of anyone on the lawn returning to their seats.

"I'm going back to watch," she said to Tim.

"Ok, love. I think I'll hang on here a bit longer," he said, accepting another huge glass of wine – red this time – and biting into a grouse.

"Sure you won't have another drink. It's rather good stuff," slurred Brian.

On the way back she went to the loo. There was a queue.

"They still don't expect us even to come to this bloody place... let alone urinate as well," said an angry woman next to her.

She finally got into a cubicle and took off her bra and knickers and put them in her bag. When... if... she ran out on the pitch she'd be naked with one flourish of her light summer dress. She checked her bum with the help of a hand mirror. It was looking fine. No smudges.

When she regained her seat Sangakkara was still batting, having moved effortlessly to his fifty. She loved watching him, power hidden in a graceful economy of movement. She wondered whether he'd be shocked by her performance. She'd have to wait until he got his century. Couldn't risk wrecking his concentration.

Tim, Brian and Chinless returned in the middle of the afternoon session just as Sangakkara was out. They were noisy and obnoxious. Brian did a silly impersonation of the Italian and they all roared with laughter, then one by one they fell asleep. Brian poured a pint of lager over the people in front of him as he dropped off.

She'd had her fill of them. She waited till the end of the over and then pushed past them, making quite sure they all woke up.

"Where ya going?" muttered Tim.

"It's a surprise," she said.

"Ooo I do like surprises," said Chinless.

"Well I hope you like this one."

At the end of the row she turned right towards the pitch and walked casually down the steps. Then with one leap she was over the white picket fence. And as she crossed the boundary rope she tore off her dress. Immediately she could feel the eyes. Everyone in the ground was looking at her including the players and the two umpires.

She knew she could easily out-pace the stewards who were lumbering towards her from all over the ground. She had been a 100- and 200-metre runner for her school and still trained daily.

Her first destination was the pavilion where she bowed to the members and then turned 180 degrees and bowed again. The words FAT and CATS had been printed large and clear on the cheeks of her bum. She had tried and failed to do it herself in front of a mirror. So in desperation she'd had to call in Clare. Having her best friend writing on her bottom felt a bit weird but she'd done a very professional job. As Clare kept saying it was the message that counted. They had considered other slogans such as 'We are the 99%' but decided the letters would come out too small and half the MCC members wouldn't have a clue what they meant.

As the shouts and laughter grew in volume she ran the length of the pitch, slaloming past the stewards. One tried to grab her and fell over, provoking another spike of laughter. She waved at the players as she skirted the cut strip – she was too well steeped in the etiquette of cricket to run onto it, unlike the famous streaker who had hurdled the stumps in front of Arlott to the vast amusement of Alan Knott.

When she reached the Compton Stand at the nursery end she stopped and waved and waited. The posse of photographers got their snaps, fore and aft. Then a large steward grabbed her rather brutally; another put an over friendly arm around her waist. They were all breathless and not a little angry at having been made to look so foolish, Pantomime boos rang out. A blanket appeared from somewhere and she was dragged and ushered past the sight-screen to the foot of the media centre where already a couple of journalists had emerged from the lift.

Cheers and boos died down as the rather jovial announcer said, "Ladies and Gentlemen, the game will now continue. Sadly the young lady will not be enjoying any more of the proceedings this afternoon."

A journalist tried to ask her questions but she was pushed away by the stewards and now the police had arrived and were forming a cordon, telling the small crowd that had gathered to move on. The light-heartedness had vanished, and suddenly everyone was treating her as if she were a terrorist or a child molester. "You're a very foolish girl," said a woman police officer.

Shouting, "Tax the fat cats! We are the 99%!" to the little knot of journalists, she was bundled unceremoniously and none too gently into the back of a waiting police van. This, she knew, was where the boring stuff started: the interviews, the charges, the court case, the stonking great fine. Clare had promised a large fee from the Guardian for her exclusive story – one of her boyfriends worked there. She wasn't convinced. The red tops might be interested in slapping her picture all over their pages. But the protest against global inequality and rampant capitalism? The British press didn't have much time or space for that sort of story.

The £1k fine would be added to her already spectacular student loan. At least she'd have the pleasure of taking £50 from Clare. But right now she was just angry... angry with Tim and the police and everyone. And a little scared.

tea

TEA
India

It was only the third time that Samendra had been to the City. His first visit had been with his family for the marriage of a distant relative on his father's side. The second was a school trip to the Siva Temple and the Government Museum. But this was the very first time he had travelled alone.

He had a 20-minute walk to the railway station. The main line to Chennai and Bangalore passed through his village. The platform was busy with people waiting for the Lalbagh Express which, unlike most of the express trains that whistled through on their way to exotic destinations, stopped at the little station. Not unusually it was an hour and a half late and the puri and samosa stands were doing good business. The local train on the other hand was bang on time and Samendra even managed to get a seat in the third-class carriage.

He arrived at the city railway station with ample time to spare. Under the shade of a banyan tree he ate the lunch his mother had prepared for him before taking an auto to the ground for 35 rupees. There was still nearly an hour before the game began and the pavilion appeared deserted. He explored a little and then sought out the changing room to drop off his bag. There he found a fellow asleep on a bench. He was a tall, slim youth about the same age as Sami, dressed in an expensively tailored shalwar kameez. A large professional-looking cricket coffin lay alongside him, putting Samendra's cheap plastic hold-all to shame.

The sleeper opened one eye and then the other. "Hi, you early too, yaar? I'm Rashid."

"Samendra. Call me Sami."

"You play here regularly?"

"It's my first game."

"Arre. My second. I played two weeks ago. Got a lucky 50. That's maybe why they invited me back. They're a funny lot, though."

"Funny?"

"Not too friendly. And the captain's got his favourites. You'll see. What do you do?"

"Do?"

"Bat? Bowl?"

"Oh. I'm a spinner."

"You're not that village boy, are you?"

Samendra waggled his head in assent.

"They were talking about you. Double jointed wrist and elbow. And you've got this mystery ball, yaar? Doosra or carom ball or some such?

Sami waggled his head again.

Two more players arrived and dropped off their bags in the changing room. They spoke to Rashid but didn't appear to notice Sami.

"See what I mean. Not friendly."

The game began half an hour after the scheduled start time. The home team batted. Sami sat alone on a seat in front of the pavilion. Rashid opened the batting with the captain, who was a short, stout and serious-looking man, probably in his early forties. His only words to Samendra were to inform him gruffly that he'd be batting at number 11.

The skipper was back after three balls. Given out lbw. He threw his bat down and complained vociferously about the ridiculous decision. His complaints were re-kindled when the same umpire gave the number three batter out caught behind.

"Did you see that? It came off his shoulder." The victim this time was the captain's brother.

The home side soon found themselves on a rather precarious 64 for five. But Rashid was still there and the crisis was partly averted thanks to a stand of 60 for the sixth wicket. The two batters couldn't have been more contrasting in style. Rashid played beautifully straight, driving powerfully in the arc and occasionally playing a classical leg glance or a perfectly executed cut or a well-timed flick off his legs. He had been professionally coached, anyone could see that. The chubby young man at the other end favoured the slog and slash of village cricket that Sami was more used to. When he fell to a skier there was another clatter of wickets and Sami found himself walking to the crease, nervously adjusting his pads and checking his box.

"No problem, hey?" said Rashid. "We put on 50 for the last wicket. Then another 50 for good measure."

Rashid set about his task with purpose. Three successive fours scorched their way through the off-side field and then he took a cheeky single off the last ball of the over. That set the pattern for the next few overs. The fielders were screaming at each other in frustration as Rashid unerringly found the gaps. One enormous six sailed straight over the sight screen. In their stand of 66 Samendra faced only five balls. An edged single meant that he was not out for one as they walked off after Rashid had finally holed out on the long-on boundary.

At tea, a few of the players congratulated Rashid on his knock. The captain was still grumbling about the lbw decision and stared menacingly at the umpire who was sitting at a separate table with his fellow official and the two scorers. Rashid ignored them all and tucked into a hearty tea of samosas, pakoras and vadas with chutney. Samendra wasn't hungry. He was nervously preparing himself for his bowling spell.

The visiting team soon set about making light work of the inadequate target. Samendra found himself fielding at deep square-leg and then having to make his way to mid-wicket at the end of the over, a walk of some 100 metres in the late afternoon heat.

"They ought to give you a golf buggy," said Rashid with a grin as they crossed.

Two spinners took over after the seam attack had failed to make any impression. The leg spinner was heavily punished for bowling too short. At the other end a short, chubby young off spinner bowled accurately but as far as Sami could see he wasn't turning the ball an inch.

"He's the captain's son," said Rashid. "Hopeless. When's he going to bring you on?"

The score was 106 for no wicket when Sami at last got a bowl. In his first over one of the openers was dropped by the keeper and the other was plumb lbw… except the umpire didn't see it that way.

He kept back the mystery ball till the second over. He squeezed it out between middle finger and thumb and delivered it with a snap of the wrist. It took most batters by surprise, even Samendra didn't know what was going to happen next. The ball would sometimes break back sharply, keep low and hit middle stump half way up… just as the second ball of the over did. Sometimes it dipped, kept low and went straight on. That brought his second shout for lbw and got the umpire's nod this time. Two wickets in two balls.

"Great bowling," cried Rashid. "You've got them on the ropes, buddy."

The hat trick ball missed the stumps by a whisker. Sami was beginning to enjoy himself. But after his third over and two more dropped catches – one by the captain himself – he was taken off.

"It's a disgrace. Last time I play for this rabble," said Rashid, loud enough for most of the players to hear.

With the seamers back on the visitors quickly hunted down the total and celebrated an eight wicket victory with plenty of overs to spare.

Back in the pavilion Rashid let the captain know exactly what he thought about Sami bowling only three overs. "Favouritism, plain and simple." "It's a disgrace." "You should be ashamed of yourself." But he got no reaction from the intransigent skipper. Sami remained silent. He could hardly bear to look or listen. He kept his head down as he changed and left as quickly as he could. Rashid caught up with him.

"When are you going back to your village?" he asked.

"Tomorrow evening. I take the train."

"So come to tea at my place. The house is not far from the station. I'll be back from college at four."

After a night in a cheap hostel and a day of getting lost in the confusion of the city, Sami thought he was lost again as he stood in front of a massive white house with battlements running around the roof and vast, shady verandas below. The garden was like a beautiful park, bright with bougainvilleas and jacarandas. This couldn't possibly be Rashid's house. He looked again at his directions. And if Rashid hadn't come bounding down the drive he would have gone back to check the street name again.

"Ah, Sami. You've found us. Tea in the garden. Follow me."

A table was laid out under an awning at the edge of a vibrant green lawn. It was groaning with platefuls of delicacies. Sami couldn't take his eyes off the servant who was attending them. He was dressed in a pure white, long kurta, white trousers and a crimson turban. He moved the chair back and said 'Sir,' and bowed deeply. Sami sat down and had a linen napkin laid purposefully on his grubby kamiz. On the white, starched sheen of the table cloth there was one dark stain which had defeated the scrubbing of the dhobi women.

"Tea or coffee or fruit juice, sir?"

"Ah… tea?"

Green tea or milk tea, sir."

"Milk tea," said Sami, wondering what green tea was.

"Help yourself," said Rashid, "The mithai and the gajah halwa are very good. They come from Vac's Pastries."

Sami took a ladoo and a rasmallai. They were the only sweets he vaguely recognised, although they didn't look much like the ones his mother made. They weren't as good either. Rashid piled his own plate high with snacks and sweetmeats.

When the tea came Sami took a sip and nearly spat it out.

"What's the matter, Sir?"

"No sugar."

The man in white passed him the sugar bowl and Sami shovelled in five large lumps.

The mystery slowly unravelled as Rashid talked. His father was a minister in the state government. He had several businesses doing what Rashid called 'import-export'... though he was unable to tell Sami what he imported or exported. Judging by the beautiful plates and cups and tablecloth it was something that made him a great deal of money. They were the finest things Sami had ever seen and he was terrified to eat off or drink from them.

"Are you studying?" asked Rashid.

"No," said Sami through a mouthful of laddoo.

"I'm doing law. It's very boring."

"I was good at maths, but now..."

"Yes?"

"Now I have to work on my father's land."

"You must go to college."

"We have no money for college."

Rashid waved at the man in the red turban. "More tea for my friend," he said, rather rudely thought Sami. The shadows were lengthening and he suddenly thought of his train.

"What time is it?"

"5.15."

He jumped up. "I must go. My train leaves at 6.30."

"Don't worry, Salim will drive you. It only takes 15 minutes."

"Drive me? In a car?"

"Yes. A car. What did you think? A buffalo cart?"

Salim was very tall and important looking. He also wore a smart uniform – mostly black this time – and a chauffeur's hat with gold braid around it. Sami and

Rashid sat in the back of the spacious Pesaro and Rashid turned on the video. Salim weaved through the streets to the station constantly sounding a very loud horn and Sami peered out of the blackened glass windows watching autos and scooters taking evasive action.

"I'm never playing for that team again," said Rashid, suddenly. He turned the video off just as Sami was getting interested in the story. "That fellow lets his son bowl nine overs of rubbish and you get only three. It's a disgrace."

Sami nodded and looked out of the window.

"But we must play together again."

"Yes," said Sami.

"I'll call you. When I find another team."

"Yes."

"And you must stay at our house next time."

"Yes."

Samendra wasn't at all surprised that he didn't hear from Rashid. He never got the call to come and play cricket again in the city. But he still played practically every day. There were the games on the maidan in the cool of the late afternoon, And sometimes a match would be arranged with another village. He worked on his mystery ball, disguising it and creating new variations.

It was nearly two years since he had had tea at the big white house. Rashid would be qualified by now. Perhaps he had moved to the law courts in Bengalaru or Mumbai or even America.

He was thinking these thoughts one afternoon as he planted paddy in the field below the village. Up to his calves in warm water with the mud oozing between his toes and the mosquitoes circling his head. The hot sun burned down and he began to dream of playing cricket in the cool of the evening. There was a shout from the direction of the village. His brother. The second time he heard him clearly. "A friend for you, Sami." And he saw a figure circling the paddy field, coming towards him. At first he didn't recognise Rashid. But there was something familiar about the way he walked that gave him away. How he had changed. Thinner and older looking. His long, foppish hair had been cropped close which made him look like a pilgrim or a monk.

"Sami, how are you?"

"But what…"

"What am I doing here? It's a long story. I'll tell you over tea. You mother is preparing it for us.

He could scarcely hide his embarrassment as they made their way back around the fields. What would Rashid think of their mud-brick house?

Rashid did the talking. "Pretty village," he said. "Your brother said you'd been in the field all day. Guess you're ready for a break. Perhaps I can help you after tea… though I won't be much good at it, whatever you were doing."

"Planting paddy."

"Yaah."

They sat under the tree by the kitchen door and Samendra's mother and sister brought them vadas with chutney and sambar and sweet milky tea.

"Mmm these are good. Never tasted better," said Rashid and Sami's mother beamed. Then he told his story.

His father had been arrested – some trumped up charge of fraud – but of course, as Rashid said, it was all politics really. Since the BJP came to power they had targeted the key Congress politicians, especially the Muslims. And his father was rich, so they wanted to get their hands on his money. Rashid had seen him only once since his arrest and he said his father was very ill and depressed.

The house and cars and everything they owned had been taken by the courts and his mother forced to go and live with her brother. Rashid hated him.

"Uncle is a fanatic, a Deobandi. He's mad. He treats my mother like a servant and he won't let me play music or cricket or have any fun. So I've decided to get the hell out of there. I'm going to Bengalaru to seek my fortune."

"But what are you doing here?"

"Arre, I saw the rail station on the announcement board. Your village. I remembered, see, and I got off. Spur of the moment thing. I thought it would be good to find you."

"But…"

"I wondered if you might come with me."

"To Bangalore?"

"Yes."

"I can't."

"That's ok. I'll stay the night if I may and then move on tomorrow. I've got no money to give your family."

"Don't be stupid. Did you finish college?"

"No, Uncle wasn't having me wasting my time studying law… unless it was Sharia law. Too expensive, the old fool said. But just as well. I'm not cut out to be a lawyer."

"What then?"

"A film star? A singer? A cricketer?… Only joking. I'll try and start a business. And I'll study in the evenings. I'm not afraid of hard work." He put his feet up on another chair and leaned back.

Sami's mother poured more tea and he announced that Rashid was staying the night. She smiled and looked pleased. He hoped she'd prepare something really nice for the evening even though they had already eaten one big meal today.

His friends were beginning their cricket game on the maidan.

"Let's go," said Rashid. "I want to get up close and see your famous mystery ball."

They played for an hour or more as the light faded. Rashid, when it was his turn to bat, thrashed the village bowlers all round the ground. Then Sami produced a perfect flipper on a length and knocked back his middle stump.

He waited with Rashid on the platform the next morning.

"Come with me," said Rashid for the fiftieth time. "You could make it as a cricketer, believe me. Give yourself the chance. You're the best spinner I've ever seen by a country mile."

"My father needs me here."

"You can send him money. You'll make him rich."

Sami shook his head.

"And you could study maths, computer science. All those dreams of yours. You'd be mad to miss out."

The train was only 20 minutes late. Rashid boarded and waved from the door of the crowded third-class carriage.

"You'll change your mind, I know it. I'll send you my address as soon as I get one. Come and join me and make your fortune.

The train pulled out. Rashid hung out of the door and waved until it disappeared from sight around the bend. Sami walked home slowly, wondering if he had made the right decision. Knowing in his heart that he'd had no choice.

Many times over the months and years that followed he wondered what had become of Rashid. But, of course, he never saw or heard from him again.

bat

BAT
West Indies

Frank is a carpenter. Least that's what he says he is. Some would use fancier names for his kind of work. Joiner. Cabinet maker. He makes and repairs chairs and tables and such. These days he gets plenty of work from all the expats on the island as well as the old money.

Wood is in the family. His grandfather and father were skilled men. They worked hard but they never had much to show for it apart from pride. Now there aren't that many people doing Frank's kind of work and he can charge a bit more. I wouldn't say he was rich, but he and Marianne live pretty comfortably.

I heard about the robbery a week after it happened. I live in Bridgetown and Frank is in Bathsheba on the east coast and somehow news don't travel as quick as it once did. The story went that Frank and Marianne had been held up at gun-point in the middle of the night. It was unpleasant to hear it but no big surprise... there have been so many drug-related attacks in recent years. The gangs are most often young men after cash and valuables they can sell fast.

I went over to see Frank the following day. He wasn't working in his shed, so I knew immediately he was shaken bad by the experience. Marianne saw me drive up to the house.

"Talk to him 'bout it, Gordon," she said. "He don't want talk to me."

I found him sitting on the veranda staring out over the Atlantic. Marianne brought me a beer. Frank refused one.

He told me the bones of the story. There had been three of them – all with guns. They'd found Frank and Marianne asleep in their bedroom. Marianne had been tied up in a chair while Frank was dragged through the house as the three hunted for valuables. They took Marianne's jewels, their watches, some cash and other pieces that looked as if they might be valuable and make a quick sale. Then the real nightmare began. One of the gang stayed in the house with Marianne and the other two forced Frank into his car and told him to drive to a cash point.

"There was a power cut, that night," said Frank. "So not one damn machine in the whole parish working. It be funny if I not fearing for me life. And Mari's. We drive all over to find a working machine… seem like hours. They getting more and more mad. Pushing me and striking and slapping. But I say what the hell can I do, man? And all the time I thinking of what happening to Mari, alone with that bastard. And then they push me out of the car and drive off."

"What you do?"

"I don't know where I am. I thought I know every road on the island. But never see this one before in all me life. I walks east, still wearing just the shorts I sleeping in. Dawn light starting to show on the horizon. I come upon this farm cottage and I wake them and they sound the alarm. I tell the police boys to drive straight to Bathsheba."

"And Marianne?"

"She all right. The fella long gone. She manage to untie herself. Right as rain." He peered out to sea again.

"I know it hard, Frank. But you got to put it behind you."

"That what Mari telling me but I not as strong as she."

"You strong as an ox. Take you time. You be ok."

"I ain't sleeping, Gordon. "Minute I fall asleep, I feel cold steel in my mouth. That's how they wake me. Gun muzzle force between me lips."

"Hell, man."

"But that ain't the thing."

"Yeah?"

"They take me damn cricket bat."

"Sir Garry's bat?"

Frank nodded. "Me father turning in he grave. He so proud of that bat. He never forgive me."

I knew how much the bat meant to Frank and his father, when he was alive. It was the one that Garry Sobers used in the first innings in the famous tied Test match in Brisbane, Australia. Sobers scored 132 – one of his greatest centuries – in a West Indies total of 453.

The bat was part of the family folklore. The story went that Frank's grandfather, Manny Lashley, had made young Sobers his first cricket bat when he was still in his early years at school. Garry's godfather was a skilled cabinet maker called Lionel Daniel of Culloden Road. And he asked old man Lashley to make the bat because he didn't have the time to do it himself. It was a good bat. And he never charged a penny for it. Garry didn't forget that and when he came back from Australia he made a present to Frank's grandfather of the bat he had used in that famous Test match. It had one signature on it. 'Garry Sobers', right across the blade. That was long before young Garfield became Sir Garry.

I first saw it when Frank and I were at school together. I was at his home – he lived in Holder's Hill then – and Frank was showing me the bat when his father walked in. He sat us both down and told us the story.

I can hear him now:

"First match of the series. Played throughout in the most sporting spirit, not like these days. Middle order: Kanhai, Sobers, Worrell. Bowlers: Wes Hall and Ramadhin and Valentine… and, of course Sobers too. West Indies first innings total set up the greatest match in Test match history. Sobers' century come in just two hours. He never play better. But Australia counter with 505 – a lead of 52. Then a fine knock of 65 by Frank Worrell and we set the Australians 233 to win in the fourth innings.

"It come down to the final over. Six runs needed and three wickets remaining and Wes Hall with the ball in his hand. Benaud caught behind second ball. Sixth ball Grout run out trying to take a third run which would have seen Australia to victory. One run needed off the last two balls – they bowl eight ball overs in Australia in them days – and one wicket remaining. Hall bowl to Kline. He tap it to square leg and run. Joe Solomon throw down the wicket with just one stump to aim at. Mackiff run out by a yard. First tied Test in the history of cricket."

In the Bathsheba house the bat was always propped in the corner of the sitting room, ready to be picked up and waved or stroked or admired. Frank's uncle Clyde, a fine cricketer himself, had taken a large notch out of its edge playing an expansive cut shot that caught the top of the big dresser. The bat's varnish had turned brownish yellow over the years. And, with the subtle change of shape and weight of modern bats, it had begun to look quaint and old-fashioned. It was a Hunts County bat, as I recall.

I didn't stay long that day. I had the feeling after a while that Frank didn't really want my company. Marianne asked me to come back soon but the next time I saw Frank was a week later in Bridgetown. He was sitting at a table in front of the Waterfront Cafe with, of all people, Jomo. I ordered a Bankses and joined them.

"Been a long time," says Jomo, shaking my hand.

"Five year?"

"Maybe more."

Frank looked shifty. I knew something was going on between them. There was always something going on with Jomo.

He'd been at school with us, though he only turned up when the mood took him. There weren't so many white boys at St Gabriel's then but Jomo was easily the most interesting of them. He arrived in form three at the age of 14. Some said he came from Canada, some from Kenya. His father was a shadowy figure, always on his travels – Jomo told us he worked for the FBI, most likely that was true. His stepmother was only a few years older than Jomo himself and very beautiful. He never talked about his real mother.

We soon discovered that Jomo was dangerous company. He had no fear and an addiction for excitement. The combination was deadly. He 'borrowed' cars and drove them with the accelerator flat down on the narrow roads of St Michael and Christ Church with us screaming at him to slow down. He climbed onto the roof of the school and painted caricatures of teachers he disliked. He traded in everything we wanted and stuff we never knew we wanted. He helped us to cheat in exams. And he was the first boy in the class to have sex and tell everyone about it. What's more he did it all on Coca Cola. Never, to my knowledge, did Jomo touch alcohol or drugs.

After school he went to sea. Sailing yachts for their wealthy owners, delivering gin palaces and catamarans all over the Caribbean. From time to time he'd re-emerge in Bridgetown, but he was soon off on his travels again, until a few years back when he returned with a wife from Trinidad and a five-year-old daughter and announced he was back for good. Since then there was talk of smuggling, gun running, currency fraud and drug dealing (the least likely to my mind). Whatever he did Jomo always had plenty of money. And he appeared to know every politician, policeman, businessman, cricketer, musician… and yes, every criminal in the West Indies.

If Jomo was a crook, he was an immensely likeable one. He was tall, fair haired with freckles and a broad, open face that was always ready to break into a smile. He never wore anything but a faded tee shirt and an even more faded pair of jeans. But his thick, black ankle boots gave him a peculiar sort of military bearing. And at his waist a wide belt with a brass buckle held a scabbard knife on the side.

He drank his coke and carried on speaking to Frank as if I wasn't there.

"When can you deliver it?"

"Monday week," said Frank. "Better you allow me few days. I never make one before."

"Right, man. I let you have the address where to send it. Morning best time."

Then with the air of a man who has just remembered leaving a saucepan of milk on the stove, he jumped up and with another shake of the hand for both of us and a broad smile, he was gone.

"What you making for him?" I asked.

"A... a coffin?"

"Someone die?"

"Not that I know."

"Then what..."

"What he going to do with it? Who it for? He don't tell me."

It was clear to me that Frank wasn't exactly getting things off his chest either, but I didn't press him. We talked instead about the police enquiry into the burglary, which unsurprisingly was going nowhere. And about Marianne and his latest work commissions. I had the feeling when we parted that Frank was already in a better state of mind.

Nevertheless I made a mental note to go and see him soon. In the event nearly two weeks had passed before I drove over to Bathsheba one humid, cloudy afternoon. When I arrived the heavens opened and I sat in the car for a while before making the dash to their house. All the same I was soaked when I arrived and Marianne ushered me into the living room with a towel while she went to fetch Frank from the workshop. First thing I saw was the cricket bat.

I was holding it and looking at Sir Garry's signature when Frank walked in, beaming from ear to ear.

"Yeah, man. It come back."

"How?"

"Long story. Sit down. I get you a Bankses and a rum coke for Mari."

Marianne sat by me. "We get it all back. Me jewellery, the money and his damn cricket bat." She nodded towards the kitchen. "He tell you about it."

Frank returned with the drinks, still smiling. "You solve the mystery yet, man?"

"Don't tell me… something about Jomo?"

"Not bad, Inspector Gordon," said Frank.

"And the coffin?"

"You on the case, man. Jomo call it he Trojan horse."

Frank sat down and began the story. As he'd already told me the police investigation had ground to a halt. But with his contacts on the island it had taken Jomo only a few days to establish the identity of the burglars. The coffin, made to Jomo's specifications, was to be delivered to the house of the senior member of the gang. Frank dropped it off early one morning. He left it on the veranda and drove off… there was no sign of life within the house.

Jomo arrived a few hours later and the coffin was no longer on the veranda. He knocked on the door and angrily accused the guy of stealing his coffin which he could see lying in the middle of the room beyond. After being pushed around a bit the crook went for a gun and Jomo hit him so hard that he was out cold for half an hour. Jomo tied him up and put him in the coffin.

It didn't take long to find the cricket bat and a big stash of jewellery and valuables. When the thug woke up Jomo gave him another slapping and he revealed where his money was kept. Then he nailed him up in the coffin along with some heroin he had found and the gun. Put them near his feet so the bastard couldn't reach them. And he phoned Frank.

"I been wondering why he ask me to drill three holes in the coffin lid at the fat end," said Frank. "We drive in the van – Jomo directing me. And we arrive at the same damn place where them goons leave me near three week ago. He banging on the lid when we drive off and leave him but there ain't no-one there to hear. That evening Jomo ring the police. Anonymous call. He inform them there a coffin at the cross road and a lot of damn noise coming out of it."

"Don't suppose the fella bother you again," I said.

"Imagine. Shut up in a coffin, not knowing if you ever get out. Whatever he do he don't deserve that," said Marianne, with a shudder.

"Only what the fella have coming to him," said Frank.

"The police arrest him?"

"I dunno." Frank chuckled. "Guess he got some explaining to do after they find the gun and the drugs."

"One thing I don't understand."

"Yeah?"

"Why you call in Jomo?"

"I don't. He come and see me."

"Why?"

"Not sure. But some time ago he come to me with an old table. It a fine piece, eighteenth century oak, worth plenty. He want me to repair it. And I did. But I don't take money for it. I say it a wedding present. Even though he already been married two year."

"And he returning the favour."

"Maybe. He come with some story 'bout being Sobers' biggest fan and he not rest till I get back his bat."

"But how he know of the cricket bat?"

Frank shrugged. "How Jomo know anything? That fella rule unto himself."

"You talk to the cops?"

"No. He want nothing to do with them. And, like he say, the fella sure had his punishment."

"And we have everything back," said Marianne.

I clinked beer bottles with Frank and put my arm round Marianne's shoulder.

"To Jomo," I said.

"To Jomo."

Marianne smiled. "Life-changing events," she said. "Sometime they seem not what they are."

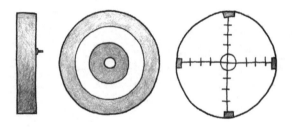

TON
New Zealand

Fear of getting out is an illusion. I'd heard it said many times. But, when I cut that ball hard over gully to the boundary, I understood it in my whole being for the first time.

If I'd grasped the lesson sooner I'd have scored a lot more runs. There'd been no shortage of people prepared to teach me, including some of the top batters in the country. "Don't be negative," they'd said. "Deal with each ball as it comes." And, believe me, I listened to them. *You'll get out sooner or later, so there's no need to fear it.* I even thought I understood them. But, until that moment, I'd never really *felt* it. Today I'd got my feet moving, I was comfortable – in the zone, as they say – and I was seeing the ball large. And then there was this extra feeling... call it concentration, confidence, focus. Strange it should happen today of all days.

As a useful number seven or eight, I'd been putting together valuable scores for the team for years. Batting down the order with the tail. I'd even knocked a couple of fifties to go with the back-to-the-wall slow twenties. I was what they call a bowling all rounder. But the chances of building a serious score didn't come around that often. As a result, I told myself, I'd never had the chance to score a first-class hundred. But now I saw it wasn't true. I'd had several chances, and I'd blown them.

When that short ball outside the off-stump presented itself I was on 56. There was an instant reaction in my mind... *over the top of gully, there's no-one on the deep boundary… give it everything… without fear.* Only I didn't think that at all, I just lifted the bat and hit it. And the feeling as the ball flew off the middle was right. I knew it was a boundary and I didn't bother to run.

There had been one big let off when I was on 29. The ball had brushed my glove on its way to the keeper, the faintest feather. The ring of fielders went up. But neither the bowler not the umpire had heard it. "Only walk when the car runs out of petrol," the great Barry Richards used to say. So I held my ground and somehow managed to put it out of my head. I didn't listen to the grumbling and sledging from behind the stumps. Didn't answer back as I usually would have. Just got on with it, and immediately it was forgotten. Now clear your mind and start again. That was over an hour ago.

The fielder retrieved the ball from the wide third-man boundary. It had bounced into the sparsely populated front seats and someone threw it back.

"Nice one, Zac," said Baz McDonnell, as we met in mid pitch and bumped fists.

Baz is our opening bowler; a bit sharp on a good day but definitely not a bowling all rounder. With eight wickets down, I was now depending on Baz and old Whitey, who was next in, to keep me company till I reached three figures. Fat chance! I'd certainly have to make sure I kept the lion's share of the strike.

"Skip says keep yer head down and get that ton," said Baz, who had only just come to the wicket.

"What did he tell you to do?"

"Give you the strike."

"Hmm. No daft singles. I don't want you running me out. If I'm going to get out, I'll do it myself. Right?"

"Fair enough, Zacco."

At least there was no prospect of the skipper declaring. We were still trailing Aukland's first innings total by more than a hundred runs. When I'd come in we'd been in a deep hole – 81 for six. Morsey, the opener, and I put on a big hundred partnership before he holed out on 97. That was another lesson for me. He tried to reach his ton with a flashy boundary instead of waiting for the right ball to come along. Since then we'd lost another wicket and the score was now 234 for eight.

The arrival of Baz at the wicket unsettled me for a few balls. My thoughts started wandering back to the farm again. That was no good. I had to put it out of my mind. I played and missed a couple of times, going at it hard handed, front foot thrust out. I was lucky to get an inside edge on a big in-swinger which would have cleaned me up lbw. I kept thinking, only a quarter of an hour till tea.

I got back in the groove just in time. Somewhere in the depths of my memory I dredged up something that the New Zealand legend, Martin Crowe, once told me. No-one played the moving ball better than him, playing the line every time. Soft hands. It was his tip for switching off and on, I remembered. *You need a fierce concentration on each ball for maybe five seconds.* He said he would imagine screwing up a piece of paper with his hand to concentrate and then between balls he'd try to activate just one of the five senses. The smell of cut grass or the sound of a bird. You can't stay concentrated all the time. You've got to relax.

Their young opening bowler came back for a short spell before tea. As he ran in I repeated the mantra in my head. *Watch the ball… follow the line.* And the clutter of thoughts went from my mind. I was no longer thinking about tea or the next over or Baz running me out or what happened two days ago.

The ball was over-pitched and just wide of the off stump. I leaned into it and followed through. I watched the trajectory as it screamed through the covers and beat the deep fielder on the rope. I held the pose. I'm not religious... but hitting a sublime cover drive is probably the nearest I'll ever get to an out-of-body experience. And I knew that was the best cover drive I would ever play.

I switched on my sense of smell. A powerful memory of the farm at sheep-shearing. As a boy I loved the oily smell of freshly cut fleece. The shearers would come. There were two of them I remembered in particular – big, lusty men, brown faces and arms. Sometimes, when they weren't working against the clock, they'd let me help. One of them showed me how to clip the wool... firm but gentle.

At tea I was on 80. Just 20 runs away from the elusive century and fearful of the effect that a break in concentration would have. I had to keep my mind clear of those thoughts.

Baz joined me on the walk back to the pavilion. "Haven't tried to run you out yet, have I?"

"Plenty of time,"

"You'll be ok. Just hang on in there."

Why didn't Bazza's pronouncements fill me with confidence?

The team and a few of the members in the pavilion, clapped us in. Freddie Morse came over and apologised for his 'crap shot' that ended our partnership.

"Must have thought I was Kevin Petersen for a terrible moment," he said with a grin. "But that's all it takes. One lousy ball."

"You didn't get to the pitch."

"I know. I got greedy. I was eying up the century and forgot the basics. You remember that when you're on 97."

"Thanks for the lesson."

Then he said quietly, "You okay, Zac?"

"Me? Fine."

"Only you haven't said much these last two days."

"Nothing much to say."

"Oh. Righto." He looked at me kind of strangely and then his eyes brightened. "By the way, did you glove that one earlier?"

"Not telling a big mouth like you," I said.

"Thought so… I wouldn't have walked either."

I showered quickly to cool down and joined the others at tea. I couldn't eat anything. I'd hardly eaten since… since it happened. I wondered if I'd ever be hungry again. I watched the others tuck in enthusiastically. The grub at Auckland was always top notch.

Bizarrely, for my team-mates at least, the conversation on our table turned to opera. Jake the keeper had a new girlfriend. Nothing unusual about that. Except this one was a bit cultural and last night she'd made the mistake of taking Jake to a production of Verdi's Otello with Phillip Rhodes.

"Cost a fortune," said Jake. "You wouldn't believe what she paid for those tickets. And it was ridiculous. You kill your missus and then you sing about it."

"Can think of a few who'd do that," said Morsey.

Fortunately the conversation reverted quickly to more familiar ground… sailing, golf and the top tips for Pukekohe Park races on Saturday.

In no time the umpires were walking out again. I was already padded up but I had to wait for Baz. I'd noticed he hadn't been holding back on the pies at tea and he began the evening session with a few uneasy prods, brought on, I suspected, by indigestion. I could have scripted what was going to happen next: a big expansive drive and the inevitable spectacle of seeing all his stumps demolished. Baz slouched ruefully off without risking a look in my direction.

Somehow Whitey survived the last two balls of the over. I was ready. They brought on a spinner and I took a fresh guard. A leg spinner. The field dropped back to gift me the single in order to get Whitey on strike. Whitey was a wily old spinner himself, but he couldn't bat... specially against the turning ball.

I defended. Then the fourth ball of the over was a touch short and I pulled it for four between square-leg and mid-wicket. I squeezed the final delivery past the keeper and took a single much to their captain's annoyance.

Against the quick I refused three easy runs in a row and the sledging picked up again. But I hardly heard it. Between balls I steadied myself and relaxed. I allowed a phrase of music to run through my head. It was the song we used to sit and listen to in the little clapboard house overlooking the sea. It was our first home. She would sing it sometimes, sitting on the veranda. Her sweet voice against the constant rush of the sea tides.

I watched each ball like a hawk as it left the bowler's hand. A nudge off my legs brought me a couple and I took a single from the next which I ran down on the off side.

The fielders crowded Whitey and he gave them a toothless grin – he always took his plate out when he batted. The ball missed the edge of his bat, the off stump and then bounced awkwardly in front of the keeper and ran away for four byes. Another broad grin from Whitey.

I was hardly aware of my score. Going from ball to ball and mastering each moment. The spinner turned a googly into my pads. I didn't pick it but I had time to adjust and flick it down to fine leg. We ran two. As the fielder picked up I knew I'd have to put in a dive. Lucky I did because it was a direct hit. I picked myself up and had a quick word with Whitey.

"94, Zac," he whistled through his gums. "Six'll do nicely."

"Three balls left in the over. Be ready for the quick single off the fifth or sixth."

"I don't do quick singles," he said.

"You do today."

"I'll be ready."

The Auckland skipper was taking an age to adjust his field. I forced myself to relax again. The vision of those long walks we took along the most beautiful coastline in the world. On bright winter days the wilderness was ours. The sea crashing below. The light through the peaks and across the moor. She once told me she loved walking more than anything in the world.

My mind stilled for the next delivery. I packed the sensory thoughts away and watched the bowler run in. He shuffled wide of the crease and gave the ball a bit more air. My feet skipped down the wicket to meet it. It dipped on me but I got to the pitch and fired it straight back over the bowler's head. Long-off and long-on were both on the boundary but the ball was struck so cleanly that it bisected them. They were not even close when it bounced once and sailed over the rope. A little more power and it would have been the six I needed.

Good bowling and better field placing and I failed to get a single from the next two balls. My fate again was in Whitey's hands.

Stranded on 98? The feeling of impotence and lack of control triggered the memory I'd been trying to push away. The feel of her skin as I dragged her from the Pajaro to her bedroom. The warm, sickly smell of the blood.

I knew she'd been having affairs for years. Lately she hadn't tried to cover them up too much but I never said anything. It was a sort of tacit agreement – least that's what I believed. Life carried on and we stayed together. I won't say that sometimes it wasn't hard. But there were good times too. Until two days ago when she told me she was leaving. I went numb. She said she was moving in with him... the latest one. She said his name: Graham or Grant or something. And when I begged her to stay she told me that was what she hated about me. That was why she needed a proper man who didn't grovel.

As she stormed out of the house I picked up the gun. It was always loaded for the rabbits. I stepped onto the veranda. She was getting into the Pajaro and I called to her and she turned. A look of horror as she saw the gun. I couldn't let her leave. I took aim. And shot her through the heart.

By some miracle Whitey survived the over. Every ball produced a loud groan from the fielders as an edge dropped short or the ball missed the stumps by a coat of varnish.

The last ball took an edge and avoided the keeper. Whitey set of for a run. I screamed at him. *No.* And he turned – painfully slowly – and made his ground in the nick of time.

I was back on strike. This was it. But I no longer cared. It mattered not a thing to me whether I scored a century or not... for I'd come out of the mind-numbing trance I'd been in for the past two days. The field came in to cut off the singles. They weren't going to make it easy for me. I tried to push away the thoughts... my last sight of her before I closed the bedroom door. Lying still as if asleep. I must have closed her eyes, though I can't remember.

The first ball was a quick out-cutter and it surprised me. I pushed at it and somehow managed to avoid getting a touch. I knew my concentration was wavering disastrously and the ball was darting around again. I gritted my teeth and repeated the mantra... *Watch the ball.* It was over pitched. I drove hard between mid-on and extra-cover. It flew in the air for the first 20 metres or so – but it fell safely. We ran two and the applause began before I raised my bat.

Whitey came down the pitch, arms open in congratulations. I heard someone from the pavilion shout, "Well batted, Zacco." I turned to wave my bat. And saw the two police cars driving up the track behind the pavilion. I hesitated for a moment and then walked towards them.

Sooner or later you have to get out.

hit

HIT
Pakistan

Abbas took three buses to the ground. One to Taxila where he waited for the express bus to the city stand and then the local to Pindi Cricket Club. At least one of them was always late, so he usually gave himself three hours for the journey. Today it had taken nearly four and he rushed into the changing room just as the last of his team mates were emerging to take to the field.

"Shahbaz lost the toss. We're fielding," said Wasi, who was always the slowest to get changed.

The captain was already marshalling his players out in the middle but he turned back when he saw Abbas.

"Next time you're late, Abbas, you'll be disciplined. Okay?"

"But…"

"No time for buts. Get yourself out here quick. I want you to take the second over."

Abbas had never liked Shahbaz Khan. He was rude and overbearing, particularly to the younger guys. Though the fact that all the other players poked fun at the skipper behind his back was some consolation. Shahbaz was a good bat and a wily tactician but it was difficult to have respect for a man who was fat, unpleasant and had a silly moustache and appallingly bad breath. Just watching him slurp down his tea was enough to make you want to throw up. However, it wasn't Shahbaz's personal shortcomings that bothered Abbas so much as the nagging feeling that he couldn't trust him… though until that afternoon he couldn't have said why.

He changed quickly and was out on the field in time for Javed's opening over. As usual the wicket was slow and you had to work hard to find bounce and movement. Javed bowled a short ball that sat up and the opposition opened their account with a four which Abbas had to chase all the way to the boundary. It got him quickly warmed up.

At the end of the over, Shahbaz threw him the ball and placed the field with his characteristic officiousness. Abbas tried to concentrate. He marked out his run carefully. But he wasn't happy with the early results. He got plenty of pace but the ball wasn't coming out quite right and he was off target. He just about got away with it in the first over… conceding only five runs including a leg-side wide. He was walking in from long-leg, planning his next six balls when Shahbaz caught up with him and took him by the arm.

"Second ball you bowl a no-ball, yaah?" Abbas looked at him in dumb amazement. He detected the waft of sour breath.

"Understood?"

"But…"

"A no-ball. And make sure you overstep properly."

"Why?"

"Don't argue. I'll explain later. Be sure you do it, boy, or your cricket days are over."

His mind was in turmoil. He had never even thought of disobeying an order from the captain before. But this was different. It didn't make any sense. He fired down a quick, short-of-a-length delivery and the batter played and missed.

"Bowling, Abb," shouted Kamil Ali from behind the stumps.

He walked back to his mark. The captain caught his eye and nodded meaningfully. He ran in and stretched out his right leg as he landed. He calculated that he must have over-stepped by almost half a metre. The umpire wasn't going to miss that.

"No-ball." The hand went up.

He walked back and pointedly adjusted his mark. He was angry now. The batter widened his stance, waiting for the free hit. Abbas fired down a short 'throat ball', fast and nasty. The batter jerked backwards and finished on his backside as the keeper jumped high to take the ball.

Shahbaz was alongside him again, accompanying him back to his mark with an arm around his shoulder.

"Good. Well done. Now the sixth ball of the over is a leg-side wide. Okay?"

"Look, what's going on?"

"I told you not to worry. I'll explain later, yaar."

"Why not now?"

"Later. There'll be something in it for you."

"What?"

"A nice surprise." Shahbaz gave him a sickly smile.

Abbas cleaned up the opener with his fifth ball. It sent middle stump cartwheeling. He celebrated by running with arms spread out like a hawk, just as his hero Shoaib Akhtar used to do. This was what he played cricket for: the sight of the bails flying, the look of bemusement on the face of the batter, the roar of victory.

He was so pumped up that he nearly forgot the skipper's instructions. It flashed into his mind as he was running in and he dipped his shoulder and sent the ball scudding down the leg side for a wide.

Between innings he sought out Shahbaz.

"Fine bowling, Abbas," said the captain. He'd taken three for 28 off seven overs.

"So are you going to tell me what this is all about?"

Shahbaz led him away from the pavilion and they stood in the shade of the sight screen. "You were being tested."

"Tested? Tested for what?"

"People are taking an interest in you. They think you have a big future."

"A big future bowling no-balls and wides?"

"Have you heard of Usman Kadir?"

"The agent? Yeah." Everyone had heard of Usman. He had half the Pakistan team on his books.

"He wants to meet you. Next week, in Karachi. And he asked me to give you this." Shahbaz handed him a bulging, blank envelope. "Open it in private after you've left the ground. And don't talk to anyone about it."

That was all Shahbaz had to say. Abbas went to the lavatory and tore open the envelope. It contained 25,000 rupees in crisp 100R notes.

The team for the weekend game was usually announced three days in advance by text. Abbas received the news he was selected to play in Karachi with mixed feelings. Naturally he wanted to be in the team. He hadn't missed a game all season and he was bowling better and faster than ever before. The winter weight training was definitely paying off... given him an extra yard of pace. He loved bowling fast. It was the best thing in the world when you got everything right... the run up, the rhythm, the delivery stride, the wrist action.

But the business with the money cast a dark shadow. His first instinct had been to return the envelope to Shahbaz Khan. But then he decided to hold on to it until he could get to the bottom of the business with Usman Kadir in Karachi. And now he had given 10,000Rs to his mother. She needed the cash. His father had been away in Qatar for over a year, working on one of the new stadiums for the football world cup. They survived on the money he sent home... and it wasn't a lot. In spite of the dangerous work he was paid far less than expected. He told them his passport had been taken away by the developer and he wouldn't be allowed home till the contract was ended.

With five children still at school – Abbas was the oldest of eight – his mother struggled to make ends meet. Abbas knew it was his job to support her while his dad was away. He made up some story for her that the money was a bonus from the sponsors for his bowling performance this season. He didn't expect her to believe it but she asked no questions.

There was no love lost between the Karachi and Pindi boys. Put in on a slow wicket the visiting side was pegged back by accurate bowling and then lost wickets at regular intervals. Their total of 185 for eight would have been a lot worse but for a final flurry of runs at the end. Wasi held the tail together and finished on 53 not out.

When the Karachi innings began Abbas struck early. Working up a good rhythm he took two wickets in his first three-over spell – an lbw and a catch by the keeper from a ball that seamed away perfectly off a length. He knew he was bowling fast when the keeper and slips all took a couple of steps back.

Shahbaz had taken to bowling him in short three-over bursts and Karachi were recovering on 111 for four when Abbas was brought back for his second spell. Coming in from the far end this time, it didn't take him long to realise that the ball was reversing. Two away swingers on a perfect length had the Karachi skipper groping for the ball. Then he played on to a fast in-dipping yorker. The next ball was dropped at first slip and then another unplayable short-of-a-length in-cutter looped off the bat handle to the keeper.

In the Karachi dressing room panic started to set in. You could see from the look in the batters' eyes that no-one was keen to face Abbas. Four balls of his next over screamed past the outside edge. The fifth swung the other way... plumb lbw. The batter walked before the umpire raised his finger. He cleaned up the new batsman first ball with an unplayable yorker. Then he got over excited and bowled a wide for the hat-trick ball.

Karachi had slumped to 124 for eight and there was no coming back. Abbas bowled one more over – a maiden. He was disappointed, not to say annoyed, to be taken off by Shahbaz. But nonetheless the spinners picked off the last two wickets cheaply.

It was their first win in Karachi for four years and there was plenty to celebrate in the away team changing room after the game.

"You were immense, Abb," said Kamil Ali. "But what have you done to my hands?" He showed Abbas his palms, stung red by the constant pummelling of the ball."

"Apologies for the dropped catch, Abb. I didn't see it," said Wasi.

"You're getting too old for the slips," said Bashir, the leg spinner. "I think I'll be taking over from you next game."

They all laughed. At 37, Bashir was the oldest player in the team apart from Shahbaz. He was definitely the slowest mover, too and his short-sightedness didn't help.

"Get an eye test before you apply for the job," said Wasi.

Before showering Abbas went out to check the scorecard. There it was in black and white… ten overs, six for 24. His best ever first-class figures.

"Most impressive, lad," boomed a deep voice behind him.

He turned to see Shahbaz and, standing next to him, a tall man of dark complexion with a crooked smile. It was he who had spoken. Abbas had never met Usman Kadir but he recognised him immediately from the photographs.

"Best fast bowling I've seen since Shoaib was in his prime," said Usman. "There was fear in their eyes today." Shahbaz grinned and nodded enthusiastically like a lap dog receiving a biscuit.

Usman Kadir was immaculately dressed in a dark suit with a perfectly presented Karachi Club tie and a matching handkerchief flopping out of his top pocket. He had the confidence of a man who knows his wealth and stature.

"I'm going to invite you to join us this evening, Abbas. I've got an interesting proposition for you. I think you'll like it."

"But I…"

"You haven't any other plans, have you?"

"No. But I want to ask you something…"

"Can it wait? Till later?"

"Well, eh…"

"Good. I look forward to talking to you at the club. Shahbaz will bring you along after you've changed."

He turned and strolled off. Shahbaz scurried after him after shooting a don't-keep-me-waiting look over his shoulder at Abbas.

The club was close to the harbour, looking out over the mangrove swamps, though in the darkness all Abbas could see was the twinkle of lights from the bunder boats and the distant glow of the port and the container ships further out at anchor. It was remarkably tranquil after the commotion of the busy streets of Karachi.

But the scene that greeted Abbas as they entered the club was far from tranquil. Loud Bollywood music, dancing girls, men drinking alcohol, clapping and leering at the girls, the shouts of the waiters, the clink of glasses. He had a hazy idea of the existence of places like this from the pirated Indian DVDs his friends had shown him. But not in Pakistan! Never had he expected to find a drinking club in the heart of a Pakistani city.

As Shahbaz ushered him to a table by the dance floor, he was still staring about in a state of shock. There sat Usman Kadir, deep in conversation with two other men. One was lean, with the pock-marked face of a TV gangster, the other, chubby faced and smiling, appeared to be the main focus of attention. Shahbaz introduced Abbas and he shook hands with Shakeel and Ibrahim and finally Usman who winked at him and appeared to be in very good spirits.

"Whisky?" said Ibrahim, the chubby faced one. He was immaculately dressed: an expensive grey suit with a white shirt open at the neck. He pushed a half-full bottle and a glass in Abbas's direction.

"No I don't… training," mumbled Abbas, who had never touched alcohol in his life.

"Of course," Ibraham stood up and beckoned to a waiter. He was taller than he first appeared and Abbas felt that all eyes were upon him. When the waiter approached, Ibrahim politely ordered a variety of soft drinks.

"Usman tells me you are our next Rawalpindi Express," he said to Abbas with a pleasant smile.

"Well, I…"

"Only we hope when you are an international star you'll be a little more reliable than Shoaib Aktar," said Usman. They all laughed and recalled some of the great fast bowler's more extreme antics on and off the pitch.

"You took five wickets today, I hear," said Shakeel of the pock-marked face, placing a hand on Abbas's shoulder. Abbas jumped.

"Six."

"That's a pity. I support Karachi," said Shakeel, spearing Abbas with cold eyes full of menace. After holding him in his stare for a full ten seconds, his face twitched and he burst into laughter.

"Only joking, my young man." He patted Abbas ferociously on the back.

It didn't feel like a joke. The chill that ran through Abbas's veins was real enough. There was something about this man that made you feel he would stop at nothing to get what he wanted… torturing his own grandmother would be pure pleasure.

Ibrahim smiled wanly as if to humour Shakeel and his little jokes. He seemed out of place in this company with his impeccable manners and cultured conversation. Unlike the others he scarcely touched his whisky. Just the odd sip to show he was being sociable. He didn't smoke either – Usman was puffing at a large cigar, Shakeel chain smoking cigarettes. Ibrahim asked Abbas about his family and his cricket ambitions. When he listened he gave his full attention, never allowing his eyes to drift away. It made him feel important.

Snacks were served: delicious prawn bhajis and fishcakes and chicken cooked in a delicate masala and mint sauce. Abbas realised how hungry he was and filled his plate. As he ate he watched the dancers, first shyly, then with growing fascination. There were nine or ten of them alternating on the dance floor. They were all young – many of them younger than him – wearing saris and tight backless cholis. From time to time greasy middle-aged men would stroll onto the floor and stand with a handful of notes over their favourite dancer, fanning them out in front of her and then letting them flutter to the ground. She would catch some in the air and pick up the others and continue her dance face to face and smiling at her latest patron.

One of the dancers, the prettiest by far in Abbas's eyes, approached their table. She began a provocative dance that grew faster and faster with the music. Her red sari ballooned around her and occasionally brushed against Abbas's legs. It seemed that she had eyes only for him and his face grew hotter and hotter. She had long hair and small breasts and her smile flashed suddenly from innocent to knowing in a way that took his breath away.

As she was about to move on to another table, Ibrahim leaned forward and pressed a fat bunch of rupee notes into her hand. She took them with scarcely a glance at him, turned away and bent over, slowly rotating her buttocks as if inviting sex. Then she swung round again, gave Abbas that innocent smile and skipped away.

Later some of the men joined the dancers on the floor and the girl in the red sari came back to their table and held her hand out to Abbas.

"She requests that you dance with her," said Ibrahim.

"Go on, don't be shy," said Shahbaz with a disgusting chuckle, pushing Abbas roughly onto the floor.

She told him her name was Sapphire – her dancing name, not her real name. They danced without touching in the Pakistani manner. He couldn't take his eyes off her. She was nearly as tall as him but her delicate movements made him feel big and clumsy. At the end of the dance she took his hand and dragged him off the floor, but not in the direction of his table.

"Come."

"Where are we going?"

"To my room."

"But I am with my... my friends."

"Don't be silly, he has paid for you. "

"Who?... Paid what?"

"Ibrahim. You saw him. He gave me 40,000 rupees... you must be important to him."

Ever more confused he allowed her to lead him through dark passageways, down a short flight of stairs to a little room. She turned on the light and there was a dim red glow which illuminated a small bed and a rickety chair in front of a dressing table and mirror. Sapphire pointed to the bed and she settled into the chair.

"How old are you?"

"Nearly 19."

"A baby. What are you doing with Ibrahim and those ghouls?"

"They... they are going to help me to play for Pakistan."

She threw her head back and laughed. "So you're a cricketer." She looked into his eyes and shook her head. "You've got a lot to learn, Abbas. And by the time you learn, it will be far too late."

"What do you know?"

"Believe me, no-one knows better than me."

"But how…"

"What do you think Ibrahim wants from you?"

Abbas shrugged.

"I'll tell you. To cheat. Win matches for him, lose matches for him. Boost his beautiful IPL franchises. Dance to his tune, just like I do."

"Well… I won't."

She laughed again even more raucously and then kissed him full on the lips. "You don't know what you're up against, little Abbas. Ibrahim runs the biggest business in Asia. As big as Bill Gates. Have you taken any money from him yet?"

"No. Not from him."

"From whom, then?"

"I got 25,000 rupees, I think it was from Usman Khan … just for bowling a wide…"

"Who do you think Usman works for? That's how it starts. You take the money… and soon you can't stop. Look at me. I'm 25… well 26 really. Nearly over the hill for a dancer. So what can I do? I need the money. And who else is going to pay me what Ibrahim pays?"

She began to tell her story. She was from Gujarat, a small village by the sea. When she was 14, her mother, who was also a dancer, brought her to Bombay and sold her into the bar line work. She was thrilled, because she loved dancing and she had been so bored with life in the village.

Soon she found she wasn't being paid just to dance... other things were expected of her. Men fell in love with her. They wanted more. She chose the ones who could give her protection as well as money. And then along came Ibrahim. And she fell in love for the first time.

"He was thinner then and very handsome," said Sapphire. "He too was a fine cricketer when he was younger. But his father was gunned down in a gangland shootout. He gave up his studies and everything else that was dear to him in order to seek out the killer. Once he had avenged his family's honour there was only one path ahead for him. He joined the gang for his own protection. His father had been a mere foot soldier in the gang, but Ibrahim's intelligence and charm took him on a fast track to the top."

He had already taken virtual command of the gang when Sapphire met him. They were lovers for over a year. But Ibrahim's empire was growing. He was always away. In the middle East and Pakistan and Russia. They drifted apart.

Ibrahim never forgot her. He hired her to dance at his parties in Dubai and Abu Dhabi and entertain his wealthy clients.

"The Arabs pay well," she said.

"And do you go to bed with them?"

"Only if I want to. If I don't fancy a customer I treat them like a friend or a brother and then they won't touch me."

"Is that what you're doing now?"

She laughed. "Little brother," she said provocatively. "And what are you going to do?"

"I don't know what they want of me."

"You'll find out very soon. And you will do what they say. First for money. Then to save your skin. Once it starts you'll never be free of them. You've met Shakeel. He's a killer. There are others… ruthless men. They'll threaten you, your family… they'll never let you forget that you belong to them."

"I just want to play cricket for Pakistan."

"Are you good enough?"

"I think so."

"Then with Ibrahim's help you'll have a big future in international cricket, but there's a price to pay."

"I'm not going to cheat."

"Are you sure? You don't know yet how powerful they are. But you'll find out. They make money out of everyone… the clubs, the casinos, Bollywood… and cricket, too. They control the betting syndicates, the IPL and they buy little players like you to oil the machine."

"There must be another way?"

"If there is, no-one has told me about it."

She turned her head away from him but not before he caught sight of a tear running down her cheek. With a deep breath she got up from the chair and walked over to the bed and kissed him again strongly on the mouth.

"I've got to get back. Coming?"

The biggest shock of the day awaited him when he returned to his table. Shakeel had left and in his place seated between Ibrahim and Usman was his 'hero'. There was no cricketer in the Pakistan team that he admired more. He was a match winner, he turned games around, played with an old-fashioned aggression in all forms of the game… and the crowds loved him for it. What was he doing here?

Ibrahim made the introduction and ushered Abbas back to his seat, next to his hero. Usman pushed a sheet of paper in front of him.

"Your contract," he said. "Sign here."

"But… what is it?"

"The appointment of Usman Khan as your agent," said Ibrahim.

"I… I'm not sure," said Abbas.

"You'd better make your mind up if you want to be training with the national squad next week," said Usman brusquely.

Sapphire's words rang in his ears. *With Ibrahim's help you'll have big future in international cricket, but there's a price to pay.*

"Are you with us?" asked the hero. It was the first time he had spoken.

Abbas saw with complete clarity that whatever he did next would shape the rest of his life. He must have nodded his agreement because he heard his hero say:

"Good. So now you're working for me."

Ibrahim was looking out across the dance floor with a strange look in his eyes. Sapphire was dancing to an old Bollywood love song, *Jab koi baat bigad jaaye* and mouthing the words.

> *Whenever something goes awry*
> *Whenever there's a problem*
> *Stand by me, my beloved*
> *There is no-one, no-one in my life but you*

Her eyes remained fixed on Ibrahim throughout and his on her.

out

OUT
England

It was early September. The date... the day of the week? He had no idea. The bus to the bridge was late. He sat on the narrow plastic bench not moving a muscle. Staring ahead. A week of sleeping rough had taken its toll on his health but even more on his appearance. His hands were cut, finger nails black, his hair straggly and dirty. But his mind was sharp today and he felt calm.

People used to tell him he had a chameleon face. Always looking different. That was the excuse they gave for not recognising him. In the good days Bryony had joked about it. "My, you look just like Leonard Rossiter," she'd say. Or Brian Clough. Or Tony Blair. Or even Mao Tse Tung sometimes, when his hair was sticking out over his ears. Even at the peak of his success with the county he could walk out of the ground unnoticed while other players were pestered by kids for autographs. He played first-class cricket for 20 years. A county stalwart... usually coming on to bowl first change and batting at seven or eight. A bowling all rounder. He'd taken well to the one-day game. He was talked up from time to time as an England one-day player, but it never happened.

He half noticed the girl sit down on the bus stop bench next to him. She planted her bag in front of her feet and he dropped his gaze. It was a cheap sports bag. But a cricket bat handle stuck out of one end. The girl looked at her watch.

"Have you been waiting long?"

He sat motionless.

"I haven't missed it then?"

He shook his head once and looked away... back down the road in the direction the bus would come from. The last thing he wanted was to talk to anyone. He'd hardly spoken a word since he'd left home – if that's what you could still call the place where he lived. A week ago, was it? Maybe more. Today was the first time he'd been stone cold sober. He didn't need the drink today. It was decided.

"I'm going to play cricket. Last game of the season," said the girl.

He didn't reply.

"If we win we could top the league."

The hint of a nod.

"Did you ever play?"

He glanced at her face. She was blonde with red cheeks and a keen, almost obsessive look in the eyes.

"Cricket, I mean?" she said, pointing to her bag.

He nodded.

"My dad plays for W......... in the Sunday league. That's why I'm getting the bus. He's playing today, so he can't drive me, see."

He looked along the road again trying to conjure up the bus.

"Did you play club cricket?"

"County," he heard himself say and cursed himself for it.

"Amazing. Did you ever win the championship?"

"No. Runners up twice."

"You must have been good. I'm a batter. Number four. I got a fifty last week. It was unbelievable."

He looked at her again, her cheeks flushed with excitement, and thought of his son. Don had never taken to cricket… or any sport really. Though he'd been quite a good swimmer at primary school. In his teens he'd abandoned swimming, school and pretty much everything else in his life for booze and dope. Parties, loud raucous girls, a bunch of mates who all seemed to be heading for the buffers. Slowly a curtain came down between Don and him. A bright young boy faded away and a monster emerged. Bryony had been desperate. She tried everything. Psychiatric help. Counselling. Economic sanctions. Don countered by stealing from them and their friends. They cajoled and pleaded, swore and screamed. It made no difference.

About the same time his own drinking, which had never been fully under control if he were honest, got much worse. He convinced himself that Bryony and her family blamed him… that they believed *he* was the cause of Don's addiction. Setting a grossly irresponsible example for his son to follow… that's what he imagined her mother saying. Or maybe he heard her saying it, he couldn't remember.

After he stopped playing he found a niche business in organising club cricket tours overseas and taking fans to Test matches and ODIs. He could introduce them to the celebrities – his old mates – and make them feel they were part of the whole damned circuit. It turned into a good little earner and for a few years he controlled the drinking. But in the recession it all started falling apart. He worried about the future and to take his mind off it he found himself drinking into the early hours with the punters.

He spent less and less time at home. When he was there he dissolved in a fog of guilt and Glenmorangie. The more closely he looked at the figure in the mirror, the more he failed to see the person he thought he knew. Not himself…

or anyone. His marriage started to unravel. And finally Bryony left him. Don went with her and then disastrously came back to live with his father again, when there was no chance of redemption.

"Here's the bus," she said.

There were only two other people on board. But she came and sat down next to him.

Before he could object she said, "Don't mind, do you? Only I get a bit nervous before a game and it's nice to have someone to talk to. Especially a county cricketer. Were you a bowler?"

He nodded.

"What were your best figures."

"Eight for 23."

"Wow. Do you mind me asking your name?"

He told her. The name clearly meant nothing to her.

"I bet my dad knows all about you. You must be about his age. I'm Diane, by the way."

He looked out of the window.

"Where are you getting off?"

"At the bridge."

"I go on two stops after that. The Valley Ground. You know it?"

"Yes."

"Have you played there?"

"Yes." He'd played more than once but he remembered one game especially well. He'd been 18. Just out of school. He'd scored a rapid fifty and hit the winning runs off the last ball. They needed three. He swung the final delivery over the mid-wicket boundary. Running wild, throwing his bat in the air and whooping for joy. For a second the thrill of it returned. Then the bleakness came over him again.

"Imagine if I could knock another 50 today. How amazing would that be? It's not an easy wicket, though. Specially at this time of year."

"You need to get on the front foot."

"Yeah. That's what our coach says. Maybe you could..." She left it hanging. Maybe you could... come and give us some tips, share your experience, coach us. Forget it! Forget all of that. It was finished.

There was his bus stop. He got up.

"Bye. And thank you," she said.

"What for?"

"Listening to me."

"Good luck... with the game."

"Thanks."

As he walked onto the bridge the sun came out briefly, lighting up the boats scudding in the brisk breeze and the trees on the far bank, which were beginning to take on their autumn colours. There was a sharpness in the air, a long-sleeved sweater day with the wind chill from the east. He walked till he was roughly half way across and looked down over the parapet. The river was swirling out to the sea. It was a long, long way down. He'd driven across the bridge many times but never before fully appreciated its height. It was famous for suicides. They said when you hit the water it was like landing on concrete. Best to get it over with quickly. Not think too much. Head first.

He knew several other cricketers who had committed suicide. Was it the compulsive nature of the game? Or its uncertainty? Whatever the reason cricketers were nearly twice as likely to take their own lives as the average Joe. He would be in good company. Or bad? The French writer, Camus once said, "Everything I know about

morality and the obligations of men I owe it to football."
The team brought you triumph and despair, unity and
discord. It taught you to stick up for your friends, value
courage and fairplay. Cricket was different from football.
The team still lay at the heart of things but success was
more tied to individual efforts. The loneliness of the
batter facing a hostile attack, the responsibility on the
shoulders of a spin bowler on a turning pitch. Perhaps
Camus knew that too: he was a goalkeeper, the loneliest
player on a football field.

And now the team had gone and from the moment he
stopped playing he felt he'd lost something. What? His
authenticity? His social context? His comfort zone? You've
got to tell yourself you are enough, said Bryony to him
one day. Because you are. But she was wrong. That was
just it... as soon as the day-to-day routine of bowling and
batting was no longer part of his life he knew that he was
not enough. And even Bryony stopped believing in him
in the end.

Not enough. That's what he would have liked to have
on his gravestone... had there been one. He'd only ever
hit her once. The evening when she poured a bottle of
Glenmorangie down the sink. He'd slapped her face with
the back of his hand. Not so hard... but her look was
terrible. And he never forgave himself for it. From that
moment he knew that he didn't love himself. So how
could he love her?

Don came between them. Their love for him, their
disgust at his behaviour eroded everything. Little Don,
into whom they had poured all their hopes, morphed
into a feral beast. He knew how to exploit the growing
gulf between his parents to his own advantage. He was a

master of lies who knew how to extract the last strands of compassion and pity from his demolished parents. When Don returned to live with his father, in the small flat he was renting, he claimed his mother had kicked him out on the street without a cent (not true as he later discovered). The little brat was always bad-mouthing Bryony. That was hard to bear. He preferred it when his son and his so-called friends – addicts and dealers and slags – turned their foul language on him. Mocked his drunkenness, stole his money, pawned his guitars.

He was climbing onto the parapet when the sun came out again. Strangely he was thinking of her. The girl on the bus. She'd be at the ground by now. In the changing room getting ready for the contest. Talking to her team mates about the game ahead and perhaps even the strange man she'd met on the bus. Would they bat or bowl if they won the toss? End of the season games… it was sometimes better to put the opposition in.

His thoughts surprised and shocked him. Nothing today was going to get in the way of his decision. He would give his wicket away, retire hurt, declare… whatever the appropriate cricket euphemism. Nothing was going to stop him ending his innings. Nothing.

But he'd have liked to see her bat. Just once. Seen how she faced the quicks, and the spinners, too. He heaved himself to his feet and looked down. He had to be decisive now or a motorist would stop or call the police. He stood, wobbling slightly in the wind – inches from the abyss. But his mind was no longer clear. He'd lost the certainty. Put it off for a day said a voice in his head – what's the harm in another day. He looked over his shoulder. Just one more day…

A van went past, the driver staring at him and veering all over the road. The next car seemed to be stopping and then speeded up again. He slid off the parapet, back to the footpath and slowly at first but then with more purpose he began to walk north towards the Valley Ground.

LEG
South Africa

Lucky watched Caliban digging up the garden. It was constant trench warfare between her father's gardeners and the old Boerboel.

"Cally, good dog. Come here."

The enormous hound trotted over and pushed its wet, black nose into the palm of her hand, as if to show that she was forgiven for interrupting an important job of work. The bell rang for lunch. Caliban looked up and bounded ahead of her towards the dining room. Some things were even more important than looking for bones.

It was a long time since she'd paid a visit to her parents. More than three weeks... and by their standards that was a long time. But she had been unusually busy. Since the excitement of being named in the One-Day squad a lot of things had been happening – not all pleasant. She was beginning to think she would never get used to becoming public property.

Sunday lunch was usually a big family gathering and Lucky was relieved to discover that today there would be only six of them. Her father sat at the head of the table and positioned Lucky to his right. That meant he wanted to talk to her. Her mother was facing her, and her aunt Dede sat on Lucky's right. Ahir, her younger brother, and her sister, Tash, made up the numbers.

The food in the Shah household was always worth the journey. Her mother still insisted – even since they had moved to the new house – on cooking every meal. Or at least supervising to the point that must have driven their kitchen staff crazy. However, there was no better cook in Cape Town and the eating part of Sunday lunch was a delight.

"Well, Lakshmir," said Dede – Aunt Dede was the only member of the family who refused to call her Lucky – "it seems I never stop reading about you these days."

"That's not surprising, is it?" said her mother. "If she's going to play for South Africa, people will want to know all about her."

"I'm not definitely playing," said Lucky. "I'm only in the squad."

"Of course, you'll play."

"Imagine what the press would say if they left out our 'Leggy'," said Ahir with a snide grin.

She turned on him angrily. "I never thought you'd sink so low. Even you." She stood up as if to leave.

Her father put a hand on her arm. "I don't know what this is about. But I don't want any unpleasantness at this table."

Lucky sat down and stared coldly at Ahir. 'Leggy'– the word had haunted her for days. She had cried when she saw the article in the Sunday Sun. Perhaps it wasn't a big surprise that they had chosen the sexiest photo from the photo session. She was tall and dark and pretty and, yes, she had good legs. In the picture, her skirt had ridden up a bit and the camera had caught an almost a provocative smile on her lips. But it was the interview she was crossest about. The reporter had deceived her. The questions had been altogether innocent… mostly about cricket: her role models in the game and her ambitions with the national team. She certainly hadn't expected a sleazy picture caption which read…

> *'Leggy' Lakshmir vows to taunt the opposition*
> *with her mystery spin. But the 21-year-old's*
> *elevation to the Springbok squad will have the*
> *boys in a spin too when she strides out onto the*
> *field with those long, sexy legs.*

The article was rubbish too… about her father's wealth and her 'wild' days at Wits and her lovely searching eyes. Hardly a word about cricket.

Paola had told her not to take it so seriously. "Usual sexist rubbish," she said. "What do you expect from the press? Especially the Sun. They don't live in the real universe."

But Lucky suspected that she had made a bad mistake in agreeing to the interview and when she arrived at the training ground she was sure of it. It was 'Leggy' this and 'Leggy' that and sniggers behind her back.

"Try these for size," said the bowling coach, handing her the SA one day kit and adding, "I don't suppose the pants will fit your extra long sexy legs."

Her plate filled up with delicious vegetable samosas and chutneys. The smell of them took her back to her childhood. She didn't have an easy relationship with her mother, but she'd always come back for the food.

"No problem getting time off from your job?" asked her father.

"The CEO's a cricket fan," she mumbled through a mouthful of samosa.

"You still happy where you are?" He'd never said so, but she knew her father was a little disappointed that she'd chosen advertising as a career.

"Yes. But I may consider moving in a few months. I'd like to do some work with a medical charity."

Till now she'd told no-one but Paola about her new ambition. But for some time she had been growing disenchanted with the advertising world. It was a challenging career and she was making good progress and very good money. But she hankered after something that would allow her to make more of a contribution.

"Doesn't sound as if there'll be a lot of money in that," said her mother predictably.

"Maybe not."

"Money isn't everything," said her father. Her mother didn't look convinced.

Lucky looked down at her food again. Her mother was impossible. She wanted to introduce Paola to her family but she knew there would be that look of disapproval and she wasn't sure how Paola would handle it. Since they met – it was only six months ago, though it seemed much longer – she had been living in a strange, magical world. But she knew the time was approaching when she'd have to make some hard decisions. They were still hanging on to their separate apartments, although Paola's place was much nicer and more convenient and she kept pressing Lucky to move in with her.

It had taken Lucky years to get her sexual compass pointing in the right direction. Two unhappy years at uni at Wits wondering why she couldn't form relationships with any of the men she met – and there was no shortage of choice. And then the truth dawned. In her final year she began experimenting. Before Paola there had been no-one serious. But she found the company of gay women – and gay men sometimes – was very liberating.

Meeting Paola changed everything. She was six years older than Lucky: shorter, with the classic Mediterranean beauty of her Italian origins… deep brown eyes and blonde hair. Her smile revealed slightly crooked teeth and a sexy gap between the front two. Paola was a doctor, scarcely two years qualified and working now in the Cape townships with the poorest families. She and her friends, gay and straight, made Lucky feel ashamed about keeping her secret. They were so open and direct about everything. But it wasn't just her mother who was the problem. It was cricket.

In the world of sport most gays and lesbians still remained largely invisible. A gay South African rugby player at the highest level was unimaginable – think of the attention he'd receive from team mates, the opposition, the media and, worst of all, the so-called fans. It was the same with women's sport.

There were at least two other lesbians in the women's cricket squad. Yanni, the brawny opening bowler, wasn't her type. Lucky found her a bit scary. But Lena, the intense wicket-keeper/batter, might have been someone she could have talked to if she hadn't been so desperately shy. The majority of the squad were Afrikaans-speaking. They'd gone to the top schools, where cricket was played. Most of them were boisterous girls who talked about wild parties, heavy drinking and the famous sportmen they'd slept with. When Lucky met Charlotte, the team captain, the first thing she noticed about her was a large love bite high up on her neck. Charlotte was wearing it with pride.

There were only three other 'non-whites' in the squad. Sizani, a tall Zulu from Jo'burg, was married to a footballer and liked to dress in snug-fitting outfits with plenty of bling. A pale-skinned Xhosa called Holly was probably the pick of the all rounders and a brilliant fielder. And then there was Parvati, a tiny dynamo of concentration who opened the batting. What they all had in common was an unspoken determination to be better than the other girls in order to justify their place in the side. The stigma of selection tokenism still lurked strongly in South African sporting circles.

"Are we likely to meet any of your team mates?" asked Aunt Dede.

"No chance. We're too busy training."

"Have you made any nice friends in the team?" asked her mother.

Sore point that. Most of them took no notice of her when they weren't being foul about her new nickname. There was a clique of older players around Charlotte, the captain, and they didn't seem very keen to welcome the new recruits.

"I only met them all a few days ago," she said. "But there's Jan. I played with her at Wits."

"Isn't she the one whose father's got a big estate near Durban? What's his name?"

"It would be very nice to meet her family," said Dede.

"Any Hindu girls?" asked her mother.

"Just one."

"A good family? Does she have a brother?"

"How should I know?"

"Perhaps Ahir would like to meet her."

"One cricketer in the family is one too many," said Ahir.

"Enough," said her father. "And my children will marry whomsoever they wish."

"But…" protested Dede.

He held up his hand and, as always when father asserted his will, the family fell into line.

"And if they don't want to marry?" asked Tash.

"Then you won't have to share your inheritance, my dearest."

Their father was a rich man. Since the end of apartheid his tiny computer-servicing company had grown into a software empire worth billions. *From Cape Coloured to Cape Capitalist in less than two decades,* was the mantra he often trotted out to his friends. His children had received the best education. Ahir had just graduated with a first in economics at Stellenbosch and Tash was going to UCT next term.

Their parents' new home in Clifton looked along the coast towards Lion's Head. It wasn't the grandest of the mansions but it was certainly expensive. Her father hadn't wanted to move – he was happy in their old place by the botanical gardens and close to Newlands cricket ground. But on some things he bowed to his wife's dreams.

Lucky wasn't picked for the first ODI against India at Wanderers – the team lost badly by six wickets in a rain-affected match decided by the Duckworth Lewis method. However, she was on the team sheet for the Newlands game. The news came through in a text, while she was having supper with Paola.

"I'll come and watch you," said Paola.

"Can you get the day off?"

"Try and stop me."

"I think my family will come too. Or at least, my mum and dad."

"Then I'd like to meet them, if you're happy with that."

"Maybe."

"I don't know what your problem is. Don't you think they'd approve of me?"

"Let's see what happens. I'll get you a ticket."

"And tickets for Freddy and Bea, too. I'm not watching all day long on my own."

"Good idea. Bea can tell you what's going on. At least she knows something about cricket."

"I can't help it. If only you could have been a Formula One driver, my girl." Paola leaned across the table and kissed her.

The weather took a turn for the better for the Newlands game. There was no threat of rain but the early start and dewy conditions were always going to make it difficult for the team that batted first. And they lost the toss.

At 37 for four there were no smiles in the dressing room. But the grim silence gradually lifted as Parvati, who had been holding the innings together, put on a half-century stand with Charlotte.

Then another collapse was triggered by a run-out during the batting power play, and the tail had to rebuild the innings. Lucky, batting lower down the order than she had expected, came in with the score on 111 for seven. She decided to chance her arm against the spinners and knocked 32 off 25 balls before falling to a fine catch on the square-leg boundary. They finally scrapped their way to 179 before they were bowled out in the penultimate over. Not enough but much better than it might have been.

The crowd was a modest one, most of them sitting in the WPCC stand and the President's pavilion. While she was batting she had spotted Paola and Freddy and Bea and waved discreetly at them. Her mother and aunt Dede waved back enthusiastically. They were camped in the row immediately behind Paola. Her face flushed. What if they overheard Paola talking about her? Ahir hadn't come, fortunately, but Tash and her dad were there.

India attacked from the outset. They were well ahead on run rate by the end of the power play and they hadn't lost a single wicket. Charlotte turned to Lucky – her first over in international cricket. She was feeling nervous as she marked out her run but her head was clear. She knew exactly what she was going to try and do. Though it was a pity she was bowling against a left-hander first up.

She bowled three tidy leg breaks – off breaks to the lefty – all on a length and there was even a hint of turn. She fired the next in quicker and pulled it down short. It was scornfully dispatched to the boundary. She held her nerve. Another dot ball. And then the googly for the final delivery. It turned, took a leading edge from the left-hander's bat and looped in the air back down the pitch.

"Catch it!" She took off, dived and grasped the ball in the fingers of her right hand. Held it as she hit the ground.

It was the breakthrough. She thought she could hear Paola shouting her name and she smiled to herself. Surrounded by her team mates and their wholehearted congratulations, she felt accepted for the first time.

In her third over, she bagged another wicket – caught behind. And then two more fell to Yanni the seamer. A run-out made it 91 for five. The Boks were back in the game. With India forced to consolidate, the game moved ahead very slowly. And the required run rate climbed to more than six, then seven an over.

Lucky was rested and then brought back to bowl, from the North Stand end. She immediately dropped into her rhythm and bowled a maiden. The second ball of her next over, however, was the one she would always remember. It pitched on leg stump, beat the lunging bat and hit the top of off... the leg spinner's dream ball.

The celebrations didn't last long. The Indian captain was still there and looking dangerous. She hit Lucky for two off-side boundaries and, after a spell of three overs, Charlotte rested her again. Fielding at deep-square-leg Lucky soon had a chance to show off her pace. Running along the boundary she put in a slide to flick the ball back from the rope and save what had seemed a certain four. She gave Paola a discreet wave and this time everyone waved back. Aunt Dede unfurled a big South African flag and jumped up and down in her seat.

The score ramped up until India needed just 30 to win off the last five overs. Back came Lucky to bowl her third spell. With a top-spinner she broke the partnership that was taking the game away from South Africa. She screamed out her lbw appeal and, after a long delay, the umpire raised her finger. The wicket put a temporary brake on the flow of runs and only three came off her over. But the Indian captain counter-attacked and took 13 off the off-spinner bowling from the other end. Charlotte seemed to lose her nerve a little and made a double bowling change, bringing back the two opening seamers. A wicket fell but the captain was still scoring freely at the other end. Pressure mounted on both sides.

As the final over began India needed six runs for victory, with two wickets remaining. The captain was off strike and the first ball produced a nick to the keeper and brought in the number 11. She took instructions from her captain, missed her first delivery and somehow managed to nick a single from the next ball.

With three balls remaining the Indian skipper drove a wide half volley to the cover boundary and collected two more runs. Three to win. Charlotte took her time and adjusted the field. She moved Lucky ten metres squarer.

With the game in the balance, India's captain eyes her options. Acres of space on the leg side. It's obvious the delivery will be outside off stump. She goes for it. A step across and she slog sweeps a fullish ball and gets a thick top edge.

At first, Lucky doesn't pick up the trajectory. It's sailing over her head for six. But no… she runs backwards, getting close to the boundary rope. It's coming down fast, swirling away over her right shoulder. Off balance she leaps sideways to reach it. Gets a hand to it. It sticks. As she rolls over with the momentum, her long legs in the air, she fears the touch of the rope. Then she sees it, inches away. She hasn't made contact.

Her team mates race towards her. She throws the ball in the air and raises her legs and arms to the sky.

They have won. They pick her up and carry her shoulder high to the pavilion steps. Charlotte screaming, almost demented with joy. They pat Lucky and hug her and kiss her and then they all stand by the pavilion gate and, in that time-honoured cricketing way, politely applaud the defeated Indian batters as they climb the steps.

It was only when they were back in the changing room that someone said, "No prizes for guessing who is 'player of the match' then.'" And she looked up and saw that everyone was pointing at her.

"Me?"

"Who else!"

"30 odd runs, four wickets and the catch of the series. What more do you want?" said Charlotte.

The post-match ceremony in front of the pavilion was a mercifully short one. Some of the crowd had come down onto the pitch and were standing behind a cordon. She saw Aunt Dede with her flag but she couldn't pick out Paola. There were brief interviews with the vanquished and victorious captains and the usual platitudes about a well-fought game and cricket being the winner. And finally the presenter, a lesser commentator from Sky Sports, turned her attention to Lucky.

"And it will be no surprise to anyone here who our panel has chosen as 'player of the match'. In her first game for South Africa with four wickets for 28 runs and that amazing final catch… Lakshmir Shah is the new star of women's cricket."

She stepped forward and shook hands.

"Well, Lakshmir… or what do I call you? Lucky? Leggy? You seem to have so many nicknames."

She stared at the woman for a full five seconds. Call me 'Leggy', sweetheart and I'll punch you where it hurts. It was a close run thing but the God of Courtesy came to her rescue just in time.

"I think I'll go with Lucky. I've been pretty lucky today with my first game. And lucky to play alongside such a great bunch of team mates." Paola would be throwing up by now.

"So, Lucky, take us through that amazing catch. What were you thinking when the ball came your way."

"I wasn't thinking anything, or I wouldn't have caught it."

"And when you had the ball in your hand?"

"I said a little thank you to Paola."

"Who's Paola? Your coach?"

"No my… my best friend."

She turned to face the crowd and saw Paola's beaming face. But next to her stood her father and he was beaming too. And something about his smile told her he understood… and he was happy for her.

She said thank you to the presenter, took her trophy and walked over to introduce Paola to her parents.

CUP
Bangladesh

Barbara had her Uncle George to thank for her love of cricket. As a girl she'd accompanied him to Trent Bridge and Headingley as well as many of the smaller grounds in their locality. Once, when the family was holidaying in Scarborough, Uncle George had turned up and announced that they were going to the Festival. For the rest of the week the two of them watched Yorkshire play whilst the others were on the beach. Her mum hadn't been best pleased about it. The picture her uncle had taken of her with a lopsided-smiling Geoffrey Boycott still hung on her bedroom wall.

Trent Bridge was her favourite ground, of course. It was where it had all started. Notts were playing Lancashire and she was sitting next to a man with a scorebook and a box of coloured pens and pencils. She watched fascinated as the colours built up and he explained the precise way the match was recorded… all the symbols for registering byes, wides, no balls and how to quickly cross reference the bowling and batting scores. It seemed like magic to her. She asked for a score book of her own for her birthday. She remembered unwrapping it. A green Gray Nicholls 60-innings book, long and hard-backed with gold-embossed letters. It was still on her shelf with every page completed, the first of all the many score books, taking her up to 1998 when she finally went electronic and switched to linear scoresheets.

Now here she was in Chittagong, scoring for the England team in the T20 World Cup. It had come out of the blue. A complete stroke of luck. The official England scorer had been taken ill and flown home. She didn't know who had put her name forward but she'd answered the last-minute call just as she was about to commit to the Notts pre-season tour. Another day and she wouldn't have been able to go to Bangladesh.

Once she'd got over the surprise and the pleasure, she started to worry about the long plane journey and the heat and the food and the malaria risk, not to mention the pressures of scoring for England. Her last overseas trip with Notts had been a disaster: horrible food, a gyppy tummy and for good measure she'd had her passport stolen, too.

But in the event she was too busy to give much scope to her fears. And the moment she arrived in Bangladesh they were completely forgotten amidst the sheer pleasure of witnessing cricket's power to bind people together in a public relationship. Muslims, Christians, Hindus, Buddhists, young and old, rich and poor. The whole of Bangladesh had gone cricket mad. Large street posters proclaimed products with bad cricketing puns or fanciful endorsements from the game's stars. Cricket dominated the media. And everyone at the airport and on the streets wanted to talk about cricket. They treated the scorer of the English national team in her Notts blazer as a VIP, if not a fully fledged VVIP.

She delighted in her first couple of days in Dhaka and then the journey south to Chittagong. She chose to go by train, through the flat, green countryside, past enormous lagoons, with fishermen in their long canoes, and scrubby woodland and paddy fields. Dhaka was an assault on all the senses; rural Bangladesh was dreamlike, stretching flat and watery for miles and miles. And then the coast with rusting bridges and boats. People everywhere doing unfamiliar things on foot, on bikes, on buffalo wagons, in gaudily painted lorries. On the train – the 160-mile journey between the two cities took seven hours – she settled into her rather comfortable first-class air con seat – £11 for the single fare. Tea was served by waiters in slightly grubby white uniforms faster than she could drink it. She got a real taste for its sweet milkiness, much to the approval of her fellow travellers who also insisted on sharing their copious supplies of food with her and asked her endless questions about England. No-one had heard of Nottingham but they were content in the knowledge that it was somewhere outside proper London.

In Chittagong she stayed at Green's Guest House, which wasn't luxury but the people who ran it were very friendly and provided delicious and incredibly cheap meals. No plush five-star hotel was on offer for a lowly scorer but she was much relieved not to be part of the main ECB party. She had an almost total lack of small talk and a seeming lack, too, of that kind of interest in other people's lives which can ease the beginnings of a conversation. What's more, her guest house was perfectly placed on the right side of the city for getting to the ground, which was half an hour out by taxi.

She made a special journey to the Zohur Ahmed Chowdhury Stadium on the evening before England's first game to get to know the lie of the land. Zulficar, her ever-smiling taxi driver, was most helpful and during the rest of her stay she relied on him completely for all her travel arrangements in and around the bustling city.

Rather excitingly, her first game scoring for England came down to a sudden Duckworth/Lewis finish. In the over before the thunderstorm struck she was able to alert the umpires and the scoreboard operators to an error in the D/L par score. Uncorrected their tiny mistake could have resulted in a serious incident. But all ended well and she felt pleased that she had achieved the scorer's aim of not being noticed... although the unfortunate outcome for England tainted her pleasure.

Between games she spent her days in Chittagong exploring the city, especially the markets and the port. Once she got over the first shock of the poverty and the noise and the smells and the congestion, she began to appreciate the secret beauty of the place. She found great pleasure in the New Market, exchanging light-hearted banter with the stallholders and haggling for small gifts for her family. But, above all, it was the friendliness of everyone she met that completely overwhelmed her.

She never went out at night. Her early evenings, before she ate, were devoted to downloading all the previous day's first-class games onto her computer including all the matches in the T20 Cup. She reflected that this was exactly how she wanted her life to be: working in solitude but surrounded by activity.

After work and supper were over, she sat in her cane chair under the big propeller fan in her room and read the only book in her luggage: Kipling's Kim. The battered hard-back edition that her Aunt Mary had given her many moons ago accompanied her everywhere. She had read it at least once a year since she was 14. But she had forgotten that her favourite character in the novel, Hurree Chunder Mookerjee, the Babu, was not only a graduate of Calcutta University but also came originally from Dhaka. Fat and garrulous, yet highly intelligent and 'moving noiselessly as a cat', the Bengali Babu spy had always fascinated her. Here in Bangladesh the book took on a life of its own. She saw Kipling's characters in the streets and markets and restaurants every day of her stay.

On the morning of the England v Sri Lanka game Zulfi dropped her at the ground a good two hours before the start of play. She liked to get into the swim early – using her official pass – so that she could set herself up and iron out any problems there might be, well in advance. The ground was empty apart from the catering people and the ground staff who were sweeping and rolling and cutting and marking out the pitch. It was going to be a hot day but the sun had yet to achieve its full fierceness and she felt comfortable in her summer dress as she climbed the steps to the scorer's box. She opened the door on the first surprise of the day.

Peering into the screen of a laptop was a large man in an ample, grey kurta. He turned as she entered and gave her a disarming smile.

"How do you do, madam," he said.

She fully expected him to add, *I am jolly-glad to see you.* Because for a spine-tingling moment she imagined she had stepped into the presence of Hurree Chunder Mookerjee himself.

They made their introductions in same formal manner. His name was Abdul Rahman. And, although he was the official Sri Lankan scorer, he was a Bengali. It thrilled her to discover that Abdul was the scorer for Gazi Tank Cricketers, one of the top teams in Dhaka and had lived in Dhaka all his life. She nearly asked him if he'd heard of Hurree Chunder.

She settled down next to him in the rather intimate scorers' room which had a spectacular view over the ground. He was not quite as large as he had first appeared, just a little on the well-padded side and he was remarkably quick and graceful in his movement. They talked little at the beginning. There was plenty to keep them busy: entering in the teams' names, connecting with the ground's alarmingly slow system, checking radio contact was working with all the umpires as well as phone connections with the scoreboard operators. She had nightmares about Sri Lankan names: some of them went on forever and were unpronounceable until you broke them down into all their many component syllables. Abdul helped her with a few of them.

About half an hour before the game began they were joined by the media scorer. There were always three scorers – Barbara thought rather unnecessarily – for international and first-class games. The newcomer was Bangladeshi too he but couldn't have looked less like Abdul Rahman. He was small and rather shifty looking – probably on account of his alarmingly crossed eyes. He had a straggly black beard and a Bengali lace cap perched on top of his head. He took his seat on the far side of Abdul, whom he evidently knew from previous encounters. Barbara felt that one of his eyes was forever fixed on her, expressing a look of horror at seeing a woman in the box.

When the game began and the tempo picked up she found herself watching Abdul in fascination. She no longer expected him to say, "Oah, that is nothing," or "I am veree fearful man," in the voice of the Babu. But now she was captivated by the way he moved. For a biggish man he had remarkable agility. She watched his fingers dance over the keyboard. He had clearly modified the software or created his own system because she didn't recognise the way it worked. There had been plenty of operating updates on her own TCS system in the past twelve months and she prided herself on keeping at the cutting edge. But this man was in another league. He used a traditional scorebook as a back-up and his writing was quite beautiful. She felt a little ashamed of the rather spidery script she used on her own score sheets.

She said nothing as she worked and concentrated. He made the occasional comment about the umpires' signals and the slowness of scoreboard operators. The Sri Lankan innings began in controversy with a perfectly good catch that was referred to the DRS and ruled not out. She lived by technology but its downside was that sometimes a request for clarification resulted in even greater confusion. That was just the start of England's woes in the field. A missed catch followed and then a bungled run-out, more fumbles and drops and no balls.

Abdul seemed to have a sixth sense in anticipating the umpires' signals: a six from the bat of Jayawardene, a wide, a no-ball. He acknowledged them with a firm finger pressed on the light button. If he supported Sri Lanka in the contest he kept his thoughts entirely to himself. She liked that. She always felt uncomfortable if the opposition scorer was too partisan, like that man from Essex.

Jayawardene was out on 89 and by then it was clear that Sri Lanka were heading for a formidable total. As always with high scoring T20 games there was scarcely a moment to reflect on what was happening on the pitch. The frenzy of data kept her in a state of constant concentration. She always prided herself on her accuracy but, for some reason, today it was even more important that she didn't make a single mistake.

At the break after they had cross-checked their scores, Abdul stood up for the first time. He was slightly taller than her and a little hunch backed. But he moved with a languid grace and stood back politely to let her out of the box first. The media scorer remained in his seat and got out a large flask of tea. He looked Barbara up and down with some distaste.

She wasn't what some of the young male cricketers she encountered would call 'fit'. Her nose was on the large size and she had slightly poppy eyes and rather boring mousy hair which was difficult to control. But her face was pleasant, her smile friendly and she kept herself trim with hill walking and yoga.

Abdul suggested a cup of tea. He knew a little kiosk on the edge of the ground that wouldn't be too busy.

"How long have you been scoring for England, Barbara?" he asked, when they settled down at an open-air bench with their hot, sweet cups of milky tea. It was strange to hear her name pronounced so carefully with that singing local accent.

"This is only my second game." She explained her eleventh hour appointment and went on to tell him more about her life than perhaps she first intended. He listened carefully, occasionally waggling his head in that characteristic Asian way which she had at first found so amusing.

"This is the very first time for me that I am seeing a woman scoring," he said suddenly. And then quickly added with a tinge of embarrassment. "You are very good," and sounded quite like the voice of the Babu that Barbara carried in her head.

"Thanks," she said, blushing a little. "But I'm fascinated by the way you've got everything set up. It's so quick and er… different"

"I have been writing programs for cricket for many years. It is my big interest. My friends tell me that it is a little peculiar. But I like it."

She smiled. "I like it too. You must show me how it works."

"I should love to very much."

They returned to the scorers' box only just in time to see the umpires emerge for the second innings. Abdul apologised for nearly making them late. He said he had lost track of the time. The media scorer looked on disapprovingly, as if he had just eaten something distasteful.

The England run chase didn't begin well. In pursuit of a massive 190 they were 0 for two by the end of the first over, and on their way to an embarrassing defeat which would almost certainly result in their exit from the competition. Barbara was counting on the team getting through to the knockout phase to extend her stay in Bangladesh into another week. But now it was looking odds-on an early flight home.

But there are times when cricket takes the inevitable and the probable and stuffs them unceremoniously in the dustbin of history. Alex Hales calmly delivered a few boundaries and, with Eoin Morgan, he began to haul back the initiative against the spinners. Then Hales moved up a gear. She had watched young Alex mature as a fine cricketer at Trent Bridge and she knew he was an explosive hitter but today his batting was in another league. One of his sixes flew towards their open window and she and Abdul instinctively ducked and then laughed at their nervous over-reaction. The media man looked at them scornfully.

The score mounted so quickly that it took all her concentration to keep pace with the bowling changes, the power plays, the umpires' signals. Hales's forensic dissection of the field and the power of his blows were positively distracting. Abdul missed a leg-bye signal and she had to tell him about it. He didn't seem the least bit put out.

By the time Morgan holed out, England were unimaginably slight favourites. She looked across at Abdul. He was a picture of concentration. But what was he doing?

"Are you recording all the field placings?" she asked in amazement.

"Yes. It is a simple development I have here. It helps with my analysis."

She liked the way he said development with a long 'lop' in the middle. "So you can tell where every fielder stood for every match you score."

"Yes. And where they are taking the catches and where the run-out throws are coming from."

Another huge six flew off Hales's bat.

"He is very good," said Abdul. "I never see him bat before."

"He plays for Nottinghamshire."

"Where you are coming from?"

"Yes I have seen him bat many times."

"So for that reason I will always be remembering today," said Abdul, somewhat mysteriously.

Two more massive sixes in the penultimate over and Hales ended the game in England's favour with four balls to spare. Barbara clapped him off the field politely and smiled at Abdul to indicate that she was pleased with the victory but not in a fanatical sort of way. They double checked their figures. Everything tallied. Not a bye or a wide out of place. The media scorer, after discovering that he had attributed one over to the wrong bowler, left without acknowledging her. Abdul laughed.

"He a very rude man."

She began to pack up her things. He stood up and she prepared herself to bid him farewell. She remembered cherishing a faint hope that Sri Lanka might play England again in the knock out phase of the competition and that she would share another three or four hours with Abdul. She was about to say something like… I hope we meet again, when Abdul cleared his throat noisily.

"You are still wanting to see how this thing is working?" He nodded in some confusion at his lap top and avoided her gaze.

"Very much."

"Then maybe you like to come to my hotel?" His eyes widened as he realised exactly what he had said. "I mean… if…"

"My driver can take us there," she said. "He's waiting for me outside."

"That is kind. I am coming here in an auto rickshaw which is very smelly in the traffic. Most specially at this time of day when it is getting so hot."

"Zulfi has air conditioning."

"Zulfi?"

"Zulficar. The driver. You'll like him."

As they approached the city Abdul began to direct Zulfi to his hotel. She realised that it couldn't be one of the bigger establishments because Zulfi had clearly never heard of it and he knew his way around Chittagong exceptionally well. Even so she was a little surprised when they pulled into a mud track of a side street and came to a halt outside a scruffy building with a flashing neon light announcing the 'HOT L FAT MA'.

"I can stay with my sister family in Chittagong," explained Abdul. "But too many children. Very noisy. So I am staying here. Not expensive. Do you have children?"

"Me? Heavens no. I'm not married."

"Nor I am. Maybe some day," he blushed a little.

He became more flustered as she told Zulficar that she would call him later and they walked into the hotel lobby which was no more than a corridor gaudily decorated in green and gold. A very fat man sat behind the reception desk and didn't even glance up when they walked in.

"Maybe it is better I show you the program here," said Abdul, beckoning to a hard wooden bench and a grubby looking table.

She looked him in the eyes. "Your room could hardly be less comfortable."

He smiled. "Very good. Follow me, please."

The room was dark and he opened the shutters to reveal a small whitewashed space with a single bed, a table and a chair. But it was clean and fresh smelling.

"Please sitting down," said Abdul, indicating the chair. "I am going and asking for tea." He left her alone with her thoughts.

She found herself in a hotel room occupied by a man she had met only a few hours ago in a country where any contact between single men and women was practically taboo. Yet she felt completely comfortable and unthreatened. Although she knew virtually nothing about Abdul she was ready to wager that he was 100% honest and trustworthy. He shared her greatest passion and he was clearly a person she could learn from. In short, she was immensely glad to be here.

Abdul returned and shortly after there was a knock at the door and a small boy in a grubby white panjabi stood there with a tray of tea and a large plate of samosas.

"Maybe you are a little hungry?" said Abdul. "These are very safe for you. I know the lady who make them."

After the tea, Abdul pulled up the bed to join her at the table and began to demonstrate the mysteries of his system. She watched with growing admiration, gasping at the speed of operation and breadth of data that he could retrieve. He promised to copy part of the software for her to load onto her computer.

Then they played a game that they invented between them. She asked him questions... more and more obscure ones as the game progressed. And he dredged through the data on his computer for an answer:

Who scored a century off the least number of balls in an international T20?

Who bowled the record number of wides in an ODI?

Who was the last person to be caught at leg slip in a Test match?

They laughed at the answers and the speed with which he retrieved them. The weight of information contained in that little laptop seemed almost magical, even to an experienced scorer like herself.

Suddenly she looked at her watch and jumped up. "Gosh it's getting late. I must call Zulfi."

As she made the call he carefully packed away his computer and tidied up the tea things that they had placed on the floor.

"Are you very busy tomorrow?" he asked suddenly.

"Not as far as I know."

"Then maybe we shall have some lunch together."

"I should like that very much."

A sharp hoot from below told her that Zulfi had arrived. She shook hands with Abdul and then impulsively leaned forward and kissed him on the cheek.

"Thank you," she said.

"Thank you."

Then he added, "I am very happy I am seeing you tomorrow. I will bring the CD."

"CD? Oh yes, the program, very kind. Thank you. Goodbye."

Zulfi drove her back across the city and she sat next to him in a state of some confusion. It had been a wonderful day. But why was she so hot in the face? Was she ill? Suffering from some unpleasant tropical disease? Or was it the samosas? She felt her pulse. It was a little fast but otherwise regular and normal.

Of course, the word love never entered Barbara's head. But she took solace in a saying her mother had often used. *You have to wait until tomorrow to find out what tomorrow will bring.*